Royals of Monrosa

Three princes, three royal romances!

Princes Edwin, Luis and Ivo couldn't be more different. But when their father, the king of Monrosa, announces his intent to abdicate the throne, they soon find themselves united in their royal duty.

And now they also have one more thing in common—their fight for true love! Because each of these princes is about to find themselves an unlikely princess. And they'll accept nothing less than governing their kingdom with their brides by their sides.

Discover Edwin's story in
Best Friend to Princess Bride

Read Luis's story in
Christmas Encounter with a Prince

And find out Ivo's story in
Summer Fling with a Prince

All available now!

Dear Reader,

I hope this letter finds you and your loved ones safe and well.

Life recently has been hard for so many of us and I hope you can find a happy break away in reading this, the third book of the Royals of Monrosa trilogy.

Summer Fling with a Prince is a summer escape to the Mediterranean, where you will be immersed in the stunning and restorative beauty of the coastline.

In this tender love story, my hero and heroine, Prince Ivo of Monrosa and podcaster Toni Clarke, act as catalysts to one another in understanding who they really are and accepting their true selves.

I wrote this story during the COVID-19 pandemic, a time when truth, kindness and an open heart and mind were so important, and I hope in a small way my characters reflect the need for these qualities not just for our own happiness but also for those around us.

Wishing you much care and kindness in your life.

Katrina

Summer Fling with a Prince

Katrina Cudmore

Recycling programs
for this product may
not exist in your area.

ISBN-13: 978-1-335-56687-4

Summer Fling with a Prince

Copyright © 2021 by Katrina Cudmore

This edition published by arrangement with Harlequin Books S.A.

For questions and comments about the quality of this book,
please contact us at CustomerService@Harlequin.com.

Harlequin Enterprises ULC
22 Adelaide St. West, 40th Floor
Toronto, Ontario M5H 4E3, Canada
www.Harlequin.com

Printed in U.S.A.

A city-loving book addict, peony-obsessed **Katrina Cudmore** lives in Cork, Ireland, with her husband, four active children and a very daft dog. A psychology graduate with an MSc in human resources, Katrina spent many years working in multinational companies and can't believe she is lucky enough now to have a job that involves daydreaming about love and handsome men! You can visit Katrina at katrinacudmore.com.

Books by Katrina Cudmore

Harlequin Romance

Royals of Monrosa

Best Friend to Princess Bride
Christmas Encounter with a Prince

Romantic Getaways

Her First-Date Honeymoon

Swept into the Rich Man's World
The Best Man's Guarded Heart
Their Baby Surprise
Tempted by Her Greek Tycoon
Christmas with the Duke
Resisting the Italian Single Dad
Second Chance with the Best Man

Visit the Author Profile page at Harlequin.com.

To Liz, Treasa, Susan and so many other wonderful friends for all your support, belief and encouragement during my writing journey.

Praise for
Katrina Cudmore

"Second Chance with the Best Man is a sweet swoon-worthy romance.... Author Katrina Cudmore beautifully brought these two characters...their happy ever after. This is an emotionally uplifting story of hope and future. Highly recommended for all readers of romance."

—*Goodreads*

CHAPTER ONE

HIS SILVER-GREY GAZE flicked over her and then away from where she was waiting for him in the reception area of the open-plan office. His first acknowledgement of her arrival. Seated midway around the conference table positioned at the centre of the converted warehouse, he was listening intently, a slight nod or frown his only feedback to what was being said by the others around the table.

The group of fifteen were speaking in English but, given their accents, they were from a wide mixture of nationalities. Their exuberance and passion for whatever they were discussing was what united them, as was their body language that said they were trying to impress him. Their boss. Prince Ivo of Monrosa. Former international athlete and now Private Investment Management CEO.

His staff, those taking part in the meeting and the twenty or so others who were working on laptops at long communal tables, were casually dressed to suit the laidback vibe of the office interior that housed break-out areas with low-slung armchairs and lavish barista machines, modern artwork hanging on the exposed stone walls. But Ivo stood apart, his exceptional height, proud stature, immaculate grooming and astute, watchful presence making it near impossible not to stare at him. He had a hardness, a sharpness in every feature that made him strikingly handsome but also incredibly intimidating.

His crisp blue open-necked shirt and navy trousers were bespoke. His wavy brown hair, cropped at the sides, was swept back from his forehead. With high cheekbones and tight, glowing skin, he still had the bright-eyed energy of an international athlete. And with a royal title, wealth, a distinguished sporting career and now a reputation in the financial world for killer analytical skills, no wonder he was aloof. He didn't have to impress anyone.

Admit it, Toni Clarke...you find his cool

self-possession inspirational…and sexy as hell. And the way your heart is thumping… well, it's not just due to your nervousness over this interview, is it? Nope, it's seeing him again that's throwing you off balance.

Unable to bear sitting any longer, she stood and stared out of the window to the rejuvenated and historical dock area on the harbour front of Monrosa town. She had so many ties with Ivo, but had only met him the once—when she was bridesmaid at her best friend Alice's wedding to Ivo's brother Prince Luis. Ivo had been best man. And it was through Alice that she had become friendly with Kara, Princess of Monrosa, who was married to the eldest royal brother, Prince Edwin, now monarch of Monrosa, having inherited the crown when his father abdicated.

She had known they'd invariably bump into each other this weekend at the christening of Kara and Edwin's firstborn child— Princess Gabriela. She would have been able to handle that, as there would have been other people around for her to chat to. But now…thanks to Kara, she was about to spend four whole days in his company. The

wedding had been eighteen months ago...
but she was still mortified about how she
had sobbed in his arms...and how horrified
he had seemed.

*You have this under control. Yes, the
timing is terrible and, yes, he's seen you
ugly-cry, but the man's an icon and this
interview has the potential to change everything. Okay, so he might be the most unnerving man you have ever met but he's still
human...isn't he? The Machine—his nickname when he won a gold medal for rowing, his expression never changing, whether
it was on the starting line or on the podium,
always the same unsettling, penetrating seriousness. Ivo never gave interviews. He was
known for being intensely private. Other
journalists would give their right arm to be
able to interview him...for an hour even,
never mind getting to spend four whole days
with him. The simple fact is that you need
this interview. You need it to be a success.
Back yourself. Don't give in to your self-
doubts. At least you know something about
his life and you're not going into this interview completely blind like you usually do.*

How on earth had she ever let Kara persuade her that she shouldn't know who it was she was going to interview until the very last moment? Yes, this tactic led to honest and raw interviews where she learnt about the individual at the same time as the listener. There were no scripted questions, no time for her to enter the interview with any pre-conceived ideas about the person. But it was a nerve-racking process...especially as the podcast also involved her moving in with the person for four days. The interviews were garnering great feedback for their unique and intimate style. She and Kara had agreed that the initial interviews should be low-key, a way to experiment and learn from the process. And she had assumed that Kara, whose team organised the interviews, would keep it that way for another few months. Instead she had thrown her right into the deep end with an interview that would test the nerve of even the most seasoned of journalists. What had Kara been thinking? Kara knew she wasn't in a good place right now...your ex's surprise wedding splashed all over social media tended to have that effect.

She was over Dan. It wasn't as though she had spent the last eighteen months pining over him. She had got on with life, determined to make something of her new, if unexpected, independence. But his wedding *had* thrown her. It had brought back all the memories of the hurt and shock and disappointment of him leaving her...but also the regret and shame that in their later years together she had stayed with him not for love but because he made her feel secure. Regret because she had clung to the embers of their relationship for all the wrong reasons. Shame because she should have known better. For her entire childhood she had watched her father come and go from her life. She had known that love was unreliable. But instead of learning from that, instead of being wary and making sure to protect her heart, aged nineteen she had jumped right into a ten-year relationship with Dan, desperate to feel safe and secure. And when their relationship had started to go wrong, when Dan had grown distant and remote, she had fallen into the same trap her mother had fallen into with her father. Time and time again her mum had taken her dad back even after months or sometimes years of absence, always hoping that one day he would change and give her the love she needed and deserved.

She should have been braver in her relationship with Dan. Ended it long before he had walked away. She shouldn't have been so willing to stay in a flawed relationship, compromising her own happiness and self-worth because she didn't know how she would cope on her own.

Now she knew that she needed to protect herself, be tougher and not be so emotionally vulnerable. In the past she had always worn her heart on her sleeve, overly confident of other people's loyalty and friendship. But all of that had been shattered when in the aftermath of her relationship with Dan ending, colleagues—who she had considered friends—in the television production company they both worked in had distanced themselves from her. It shouldn't have been such a surprise. After all, Dan was the global star of riveting historical documentaries and the reason why the production company's fortunes were growing year on year. She, as a producer, was much more replaceable. Even if it was her who introduced Dan to the production company in the first place when they had been searching for a presenter of their new documentary series.

Never again would she allow herself to be hurt. Yes, she dated guys but she kept them at a distance. She had no interest in anything serious and was instead pouring her energy into her career as a podcaster.

This *YA Together, Person Unknown* podcast was everything to her. It was her way of re-establishing her name and reputation. It was the thing that gave her a purpose in life. She could *not* mess up this golden opportunity.

Along the marina, office workers finished for the week, and, no doubt celebrating the fact that it was a long weekend in Monrosa, as Monday was a national holiday, sat outside the bars and cafés, sipping cocktails and eating tapas. Her stomach grumbled. She hadn't eaten since she had grabbed a croissant in her local café this morning on the way to the airport. But she hadn't even managed to eat that in full, thanks to Kara's phone call. Kara had excitedly announced that she had set her up with an interview for the weekend. Toni had argued that she was in no fit state to interview anyone but Kara wasn't having any of it. Kara wouldn't even listen to her protests that she had been looking forward to spending the weekend getting to know Gabriela. Instead Kara had ended the call saying that as usual the driver who was to collect her at the airport would inform her of her interviewee once they were approaching the interviewee's place of work. She had binned her croissant and run home to collect her portable recorder and microphones.

'Miss Clarke?'

She swung around, her heart pounding. She hadn't heard him approach.

'My apologies for keeping you waiting.' He gestured in the direction of the refreshment area. 'Can I get you something to drink?'

He was so polite, so formal. So unperturbed at meeting her again. Blood rushed to her cheeks. His voice, deep and accented, had her heart thumping in her chest.

'No, thank you, Your Highness.'

He asked her to follow him and, grabbing her laptop bag, she followed him into one of the glass-walled offices to the side of the warehouse. He sat behind the desk, a huge window behind him giving a view of the row of mega-yachts lining the marina, the ferry that ran between here and Monrosa old town creating a white ribbon wake in the ink-blue Mediterranean.

She took a seat on the opposite side of the desk.

He fixed those silver eyes on her. Seconds passed. He continued to stare at her. Was this a test? She smiled in the hope he might respond in kind. He didn't. She felt herself redden again, her heart really pounding now under the force of his gaze, the aura of power that surrounded him, his comfort with the silence between them that was making her want to start babbling. And what really scared her was that one very crazy and inappropriate question kept going around her head and she was terrified of blurting it out.

Do you like having sex standing up?

What was the matter with her? Why was she sitting here trying to erase the image of Ivo holding her against a wall, that deep voice whispering into her ear?

'Four days seems excessive.'

Was he thinking about sex too? She swallowed hard. 'Four days?'

He frowned. 'Yes, the interview. Kara said it would take four days.'

'Oh…yes… I'm afraid so.' She took a deep breath, knowing she needed to focus. She was used to this. Interviewees having second thoughts about agreeing to the interview in the first place. 'But I promise to be a good houseguest. I don't have any bad habits…that I know of anyway. Although one of my interviewees did reckon I hogged the bathroom too much in the morning, but then she did live in a one-bathroom apartment, not a palace.' She gave a laugh. And then cringed when his expression tightened.

It was time to start again. She held out her hand. 'Sir it's really nice to see you again and thank you for agreeing to the interview. As Kara may have explained, I do not know who I am interviewing until I arrive, so it's a great pleasure and surprise to know that it's you.' Surprise, yes. Pleasure…that she wasn't certain of.

He leant across the table and took her hand. His grip was as strong and encompassing as she remembered. Breaking away, he asked, 'Why a pleasure?'

His stare was uncompromising. As though he was assessing every detail about her, storing away every fact in order to decide whether he was going to go ahead with this interview. And instead of meeting him head on and persuading him that this was something he wanted to do, her brain headed off in a completely different direction.

Well, pleasure might be pushing it. Yes, I could watch you for eternity—you have the face and body of a Greek god—but in truth you kind of terrify me. Quiet people unnerve me. I like chat and banter. I like connecting with people and knowing where I stand with them. I don't want complications or awkwardness. But with you... I'm not sure I'll manage any of those things.

She sat more upright in her chair. It was time to pull herself together and do her job. 'Your appearance on the podcast will help us to reach an even wider audience. People will want to hear your story.' She paused, a sense of purpose grounding her. 'This podcast, *Person Unknown*, is a gateway for people to learn that Young Adults Together is there to support them with any mental health problems they're facing. After each podcast, there's a spike in people contacting the helplines. But lots of young people either don't know of the service or are too nervous to make contact—in having prominent people talk about their lives and what they have learnt in both good and bad times, listeners can realise that they aren't alone in facing challenges. I am certain that your interview will be immensely powerful in helping others.'

He didn't respond to her answer. His gaze shifted away to a point over her shoulder, a tiny movement ticking in his jaw. Outside, in the main office, staff were leaving for the day, their chatter and laughter in stark contrast with the silence between them.

She needed to take this situation in hand. Unzipping her laptop bag, she said in her best cheerful voice, 'But before we talk any further, let me set up my equipment. As Kara will have explained, I always hold my first interview at the person's place of work so that listeners get a glimpse of their professional life. And I begin recording as soon as is feasible so that the listeners get to hear our interactions from the very beginning. We want them to feel immersed in the whole experience.' Placing the recorder on the table, she plugged the two microphones in and, positioning them in their mike stands on the table, she stood and leant across the desk in order to put the mike close to him. Raising her head, she met his solemn silver gaze. For long moments neither of them looked away. A buzz of attraction danced in the air between them. 'Are you ready for me?'

He raised an eyebrow.

Heat blasted her cheeks. 'I mean, are you ready for me to start the interview?'

A single small diamond around her neck swung as she waited for his answer. The top three buttons of her yellow dress were undone, her pale yellow bra beneath visible. Her perfume hadn't changed—it was still that light, floral scent. He inhaled an irritated breath, admitting to himself that ever since Luis's wedding he had been subconsciously keeping tabs on her life, alert to any conversations Kara and Alice had about her, lingering over the media reporting of her split with her ex, newsworthy because he was a famous and much in demand TV historian.

Frowning, as though wondering just when he'd answer her question, she pushed her long brown hair back behind one ear. It was the same light chestnut colour as her eyes. Her nose was pert, her lips full. Her skin lightly tanned. At Luis and Alice's wedding she had worn a gold sequinned bridesmaid dress that emphasised the swell of her breasts, the curve of her narrow waist, and when she had walked down the aisle, her hair tied up, tears in her eyes despite her wide smile, he had been unable to tear his gaze away from her. She had a soft, gentle beauty that was utterly captivating. He had told himself that he followed any news on Toni with just the same interest and concern he would have for anyone who had an association with the family. But some nights, alone in the silence of his *finca*, the idea of contacting her would bubble inside of him… but that idea had never become more than a fleeting thought, as he had never been sure of what purpose it would serve, and anyway, the complications of contacting her were too great, considering her ties with both of his sisters-in-law.

But now she was back in his life…and he wanted to end all of this. Now. He had zero interest in talking about his life…or sharing his home and privacy with anyone.

But Kara had pleaded with him to do this interview and deep down he knew it was the right thing to do for the charity. He would take part in the interview but he would control it at all times. And shut it down whenever he wanted to. He would only talk about the things he was comfortable discussing—his sporting and financial careers. There was plenty of material and life lessons in both. Enough to fill the hour-long podcast. 'Before we start I think I should make it clear that I'm not given to overthinking or self-inspection—I will answer your questions but please don't expect any great insights.'

She sat down, still frowning. Went to speak, stopped, studied him some more, but then with the slightest of shrugs said, 'How about we just give it a go? People are sometimes surprised at how much they learn about themselves by taking part in the interview.'

He made a disbelieving sound. Her response was yet another shrug and with a hopeful smile she said, 'Here we go,' before pressing the 'record' button.

'Hi and welcome back to the *YA Together, Person Unknown* podcast, where we meet the person behind the fame and explore their life lessons. I'm your host, Toni Clarke.

'So guys, this week I am beyond thrilled with who I'm getting to interview. But before I introduce you, let me give you some teasers to see if you can work out who it is. I'm on a Mediterranean island that I reckon should be famous for its three Bs: beauty, beaches and banging cocktails. Right now, I'm sitting in the coolest office I have ever visited, a brilliant blue summer sky visible out the window, and we're surrounded by art galleries and bars and restaurants. It's Friday evening and people are out partying. The vibe here is amazing. And across from me is my interviewee. An international gold medallist and now successful CEO. I think it's fair to say that we all know *of* him, but not many of us know him, the real man. Oh, and did I mention that he's also royalty? Can you guess who it is? Yes, it's Prince Ivo of Monrosa. Welcome to my podcast, Your Highness.'

'Thank you.' Her style was upbeat, intimately chatty, and he guessed well suited to her young audience. It left him dreading what was to come. He had to hand it to Kara. She was a master at picking her moments in persuading people to commit to things. Last night she had brought Gabriela to visit him in his apartment in the palace, on the pretence of discussing his role as Gabriela's godfather at her christening on Sunday. But as he held Gabriela, terrified but in awe of just how perfect every tiny detail of her was, Kara had asked him once again to take part in this podcast, arguing that people would be inspired by the struggles he had faced to achieve sporting success. For a while he had wavered, knowing he should provide more support to the charity, given that he hadn't been able to commit fully to his role as its ambassador in recent years as he'd built up the business and taken over his role as special advisor to the treasury, at Edwin's request. But then Kara had admitted that it would entail the interviewer, Toni Clarke, moving in with him for four days. The thought of being all alone with the beautiful Toni Clarke for four days had been a tempting proposition…but his home was his sanctuary. Sharing that with anyone was a step too far. He had been about to say no but then Gabriela had started to cry. And, as she paced his apartment with a fretful Gabriela, Kara had described her concern for Toni.

At Luis's wedding, Toni had been an exhausting, exuberant and excitable chatterbox. But when they had danced he had seen a different side to her. A more vulnerable, troubled side.

'Of course, this isn't the first time that we've met—as some of you know, my best friend is Alice O'Connor, who is married to Prince Luis. When they married, I was bridesmaid and Prince Ivo the best man.' She met his eyes, her cheeks growing warm. 'The wedding day was incredible, wasn't it? But we didn't get to spend much time getting acquainted.'

'No.'

She waited for him to say something else. But what was he supposed to say? That in fact when they had danced, thrown by her silence, he had attempted to make conversation with her and asked her if she was enjoying herself. She had answered, 'I'm trying to,' and her eyes had held such a sadness that he had without thought murmured, 'Everything will be okay.' He had followed her when she had bolted away. Horrified that he had somehow upset her. And when he had apologised out in the palace gardens, she had sobbed, soaking his shirtfront in the process. Not able to get any sense from her what the matter was and at a loss how to help her, he had simply held her until she said she needed to go and call her boyfriend. He hadn't realised that she was in a relationship given that she didn't have a partner attend the wedding with her.

'It was an emotional day. Gosh, I think I cried more in that one day than I did in my entire life. They were all tears of joy of course. Weddings are such moving affairs and Alice was such a beautiful bride.' Pausing to draw a deep breath as though to say that drew a line on what had happened between them at the wedding, she tilted her head to the side and continued, 'You're variously described as being the youngest of the three Monrosian Royal Princes and an international rower. But if you were to describe yourself, what would you say?'

See, it was questions like this that he hated. How was he supposed to answer it?

I keep to myself. I don't overthink things. I get on with life and I don't spend too much time navel-gazing.

'I like to work hard.'

'And outside of work?'

'I have my royal duties and in particular my advisory role to the Treasury.'

Shifting back in her chair, she frowned and silence fell between them. Raúl, the Director of Royal Communications, had attempted several times to counsel him on the art of interviews, but Ivo couldn't see what was wrong with a blunt approach. It avoided wasting time. He had zero interest in the personal lives of others, so he never understood why anyone would have an interest in his.

'Your company Pacolore Investments has become incredibly successful in a very short space of time. What do you think is behind that success?'

At last. A question he was comfortable

answering. 'I set up Pacolore before I retired from rowing, so I had a clear view of what my business plan would be from the very start. But the key I believe to our success is that I recruit a wide diversity of people. I want people who think differently, who come from different backgrounds and life experiences. We see opportunities that other investment companies miss.'

'Where does that policy come from?'

He knew the odds stacked against those who operated outside the usual social norms and expectations. It was a bugbear of his that the confident talkers, those from a certain background, those who followed a conventional path in life were snapped up by employers. Those who were different left behind. Which was why he never followed the normal process of interviewing but instead made his recruitment decisions based on past performance and their completion of an online skills assessment. He judged people on their actual skills, not on how well they could sell themselves. 'I studied Financial Maths at university and after graduating I heard about how some of my brightest classmates didn't thrive in the more conventional investment firms—if they managed to get in the door, many didn't even get beyond the interview stage. I ran Pacolore for many years on my own while I rowed, investing my own money, making mistakes and learning from them. Through that work, I joined online investment discussion groups and I realised the wealth of talent out there… hugely intelligent and lateral-thinking people who just because of the fact that they didn't go to the right university or lived on the other side of the world, never got the opportunity to work in an investment firm. I was determined to recruit as diverse a group as possible. I like difference.'

Her expression intrigued, she asked, 'Why?'

'Because it is those who are different, who don't fit the mould, who often live on the periphery of groups and wider society, who are the true innovators and change makers.'

'Do you see yourself as being different?'

He heard it in her tone, the suggestion that he couldn't be different. How could a person born into such privilege, class themselves as being outside the norm? But in truth he had always felt separate from those around him. 'In ways.'

She waited for him to expand, her expression growing more quizzical but when she grew tired of waiting, she asked, 'Before university, where did you go to school? What was your childhood like?'

Confusing and lonely. Terrifying at times. Not that he'd admit that to anyone. 'I was sent to boarding school in England when I was ten.'

'Did you like it there?'

'I grew to like it.'

Her eyes took on a softness that made him shift in his seat. 'You went to boarding soon after your mother, Princess Cristina, died. It must have been a tough time for you.'

CHAPTER TWO

Ivo PUSHED BACK in his chair. 'I don't remember a lot about that time.' He waited in dread for her to ask about his mother, to describe her, to talk about her death. It was well documented in the press that he was alone with her when she died. Would she ask him to recall that day and the nightmare that unravelled in the days that followed?

His father's initial shock at her death had almost instantly morphed into fury—he had raged against the stable staff, the bodyguards who hadn't accompanied them on the trek even though he knew his mother always insisted on trekking with the horses alone. Sick with guilt, unable to process what had happened, Ivo had tried to tell his father how he had begged her to go riding with him even though she had said she wasn't feeling well, how he panicked and ran for help when he should have stayed with her so that she didn't die alone, but his father had shut him down, too angry to listen. In his grief, Ivo had ached for the safety and comfort of his family but it was as though everything he knew and understood in his life had imploded. His family had changed out of all recognition. His father had been furious with the world, Edwin constantly preoccupied and trying to act like a buffer against that anger, while Luis had found refuge with his friends, disappearing from the palace for days on end. His mother had understood him, his innate quietness and need for time alone, but when she had died that understanding had disappeared from his life and, though he had so desperately wanted privacy to grieve, had wanted to keep a low profile throughout her state funeral, his father had insisted he play a central role in the proceedings. And as he faced the other mourners' stares he had wanted so desperately to cry himself but knew to do so would be unacceptable. To survive he had closed himself off not only from the outside world but also from his own family. And that detachment had become even more necessary when he had been thrown into the bewildering world of boarding school, where there was no escape from others, where the only way to survive was to single-mindedly pursue the challenge of getting onto the school's first rowing eight, where he had little time to think. Rowing had given his life structure…and the perfect excuse to avoid the emotional entanglement of friendships. The rowing team had accepted him, making no demands on him other than wanting his physical skills and unrelenting drive to win. They never questioned his silence. Unlike his own family, who could never hide their bafflement and disappointment with him. He never measured up to what they thought he should be. They never accepted that he had little interest in socialising, in indulging in small talk and that he abhorred being in the limelight.

But instead of asking any further questions Toni pointed to the microphone and said, 'I need you to stay close to the mike. I should have explained that before we started. And don't worry about any of these asides, I can edit them out…and of course I will edit out any questions or answers you aren't happy with. This is your podcast… I won't release anything you or the Palace aren't happy with.' Pausing, she gave him a quick smile before asking, 'What are your ambitions for the future?'

Her change of tack away from the topic of his mother and childhood was deliberate. Why had she done that? A lifetime of knowing people wished you to be different had made him wary of what lay behind even the most innocuous of actions. His father's bribes and threats when he spent too long in his bedroom. The summer camps he had been forced to attend, the camp leaders watching his every move, no doubt under instruction to do so by his father. Edwin's poorly disguised suggestions that he socialise more. Luis's visits to him at university and later on at rowing training camps, insisting they go to the most crowded and noisiest bars and clubs in town. Luis, who thrived on chaos, could never fathom his preference for more private bars and restaurants. 'For the immediate future I want to embed Pacolore's success.'

'You don't want to expand the business?'

'Perhaps, but now isn't the time.'

'I had thought, given how successful you have been, you'd be keen to have the business grow. Are you a risk-taker or cautious by nature?'

'I'm a calculated risk-taker. And rapid growth isn't my motivator.'

'What is?'

'Obviously a certain level of financial gain is paramount, but it's the analysis, reading the markets and making the right call that gives me the greatest buzz. I like seeing my team thrive and develop.'

She nodded several times as though considering his answer, before she asked, 'And what are your ambitions for your private life?'

'In what sense?'

For a moment, a shadow of annoyance flittered in her eyes. If she was hoping for a free-flowing conversation she was interviewing the wrong person. With a shrug, as though it weren't a significant question and she didn't particularly care what his answer would be, she asked, 'Do you want to marry? Have children?'

'I have no plans to do so.'

'Are you in a relationship now?'

He had dated in the past, but it never worked out. He wasn't blind to the fact that women were attracted to him because they thought he offered a world of glamour and success. But few were prepared to accept the reality. That he worked as hard as he had trained as a rower, that he had no interest in partying or having a high profile. He inhaled a deep breath, now irritated with this questioning. 'No, I'm not in a relationship.' He glanced out into the main office. All of the others had left for the weekend. They were now alone. And would be until Sunday when they travelled to Gabriela's christening. He really did not know if he could do this.

'Why have you agreed to this interview?' The tone of her question was curious but, meeting her gaze, he saw uncertainty and doubt. She leant towards him, resting an arm on the desk, her eyes taking on a soft gentleness as though imploring him to trust her.

'To support Kara and her work with YA Together. I am a goodwill ambassador for the charity but, due to my work in recent years, I've not been able to work as closely with the charity as I would have liked. This interview is part of my contribution to make up for that.' He hadn't needed the tiredness in Kara's eyes last night or the short and pointed phone call from Edwin today to know that Kara needed extra support now that Gabriela had arrived. He knew how important the charity was to Kara and though he was a reluctant participant he could see how impactful and wide-reaching this podcast could be.

She frowned, as though uncertain what her next question would be. 'Have you ever personally had mental health issues?'

He knew the answer he should give—the one he had settled on overnight, knowing that the issue would eventually come up. But something about the softness of her voice, the gentle enquiry in her eyes, stole his answer away. And for the briefest of moments he was tempted to admit how separate he felt from the world...until good sense and the need to protect himself kicked back in. 'Being an athlete is as much about psychological strength as it is physical. There have been times when I've struggled with injuries, been dropped from the team and of course lost races. I have learnt to accept where I am at the moment, not project negativity into the future, and try to be content with what I have already achieved.'

Her nose wrinkled as though she was trying to unpack his answer...which even he had to admit was more ambiguous than he had intended. 'Where's your happy place... where do you feel most at home?'

'I own a *finca* in the north of the island. I spend as much of my free time there as is possible.' The last time he had brought someone to stay at the *finca* it had been an ex-girlfriend who had been unable to conceal her horror at its simple structure and remoteness. Was the same thing going to happen this weekend with Toni? Would she judge and criticise the life that made him happy? He picked up his phone. 'I have calls I have to make before we leave.'

This was a disaster. She wasn't getting to know him. Yes, it was only the first interview but the flow was all wrong. Her questions were meandering and without focus. And even without listening back to the recording she knew that they sounded both stiff and uptight. She needed to inject some fun into the interview. Break down some of the tension between them. She grabbed her notebook from the laptop bag and opened it to the list of questions that she had decided to keep in her back pocket in case any interview went as pear-shaped as this one was going.

'Of course. I'll leave you to your calls but first can I ask you to take part in a rapid-fire interview quiz?'

'Why?'

She needed to counteract his wariness with a healthy dose of enthusiasm. 'Because it will be fun!'

His gaze narrowed. 'Only if I can ask you a round of questions too.'

Why would he want to do that? She couldn't say no…but the feeling of not being in control of this interview escalated at the prospect. 'No problem. Do you want to share my list?'

'No, I'll think of my own.'

'Okay…this will be interesting. I'll start first. Apple or orange?'

He folded his arms, as though to say *Seriously…? Is this the level of interview you are going to subject me to?*

She winced, waiting for him to call a halt to the interview. But, raising one of those thick, straight eyebrows that emphasised the hard, masculine intensity of his face, he answered, 'Orange.'

'What couldn't you live without?'

'My dogs.'

He had dogs. She smiled warmly. 'Ah, how sweet!' She wanted to ask more about them but this was supposed to be a quick-fire session. 'When was the last time that you lied?'

'Last night.'

Her heart sank. *Please don't have hurt someone.*

'What happened?'

'I said that I was okay with Princess Gabriela spewing on my shirt.'

She laughed in relief. 'I haven't seen her yet. Is she as gorgeous as she is in the photos?'

'Even more so.'

Her heart kicked at the tenderness in his voice...maybe he did have a soft side after all. And for a moment he held her gaze and she was transported back to Alice's wedding when they had danced together. The gentleness, the empathy in his voice, when he had asked her if she was enjoying herself, the way he held her gaze, not looking away, had jolted her into realising that Dan never looked at her that way any more. And everything she had been trying to deny, her loneliness, how unattractive she felt, how she didn't know herself any more, had all collided and she had ended up uncontrollably sobbing in his arms. She looked down at her list of questions, found the next one. 'What irritates you?'

'People who do not accept or respect other people's choices.'

She studied him, but the tightening of his mouth told her not to follow up what he meant by that…not yet at least. 'Your most embarrassing moment?'

'Catching a crab while competing in the world junior championships and ending up in the water.'

She frowned. 'An actual crab made you fall out of the boat?'

He stared at her and then the most wonderful smile played on his lips. 'No, it's the expression used in rowing when the oar blade gets caught in the water.'

'Oh.' She rolled her eyes. And was re-warded with the pleasure of seeing soft amusement glisten in his eyes. 'Beer or wine?'

'Wine.'

'Do you have a motto?'

'No.'

'If you did, what would it be?'

He rolled his neck, considering this. 'I guess…be true to yourself.'

'Have you ever been heartbroken?'

He rubbed his hand along his jaw, shrugged. 'Upset…' he paused, his eyes holding hers, his voice dropping a notch '…but not heartbroken.'

She was glad. For his sake. 'What makes you happy?'

'Walking with my dogs late at night in the olive groves surrounding my *finca*.'

'Why?'

'I don't know… I guess the silence there and the fact that there are no expectations or pressure on me at that time.'

Was he talking about the pressures of work, or those that came from his royal duties? There was so much more she wanted to ask him, but she knew she had to bide

her time. Ivo was the most reluctant interviewee she had ever had. She needed to
build his trust in her. She needed to be pa-
tient. He was deep and complicated, a man
you might never fully know. She shut her
notebook. 'That's all my questions—now
it's your turn.'

He nodded, frowning in thought before
he asked, 'Pear or pineapple?'

'Pear to eat, pineapple in a cocktail.'

'Town or country?'

'Definitely town.'

He shrugged at her answer as though he
had expected as much. 'What one word
would you use to describe yourself?'

'Curious.'

'Olive oil drizzled on ice cream—yes or
no?'

She pretend-gagged. 'Definitely no—is
that even a thing?'

'You haven't even tried it? I'll make it for
you this weekend.' Ignoring her look of horror, he continued, 'Cocktails on the beach
or hiking in the mountains?'

'That's an easy one—cocktails on the
beach.'

There it was again, that shrug that said

she wasn't surprising him. Did he disap-
prove of any form of slacking? What did
she expect—he was an ex-international athlete and now an investment manager. That
profile wouldn't exactly suggest someone
who could chill out easily. Did he enjoy life?
Party? Find ways to escape from reality for
a while?

'What second word would you use to describe yourself?'

Without thinking she answered, 'Thin-
skinned.'

She gave a laugh, trying to pretend she
was kidding, but Ivo didn't even crack a
smile in return. Instead he asked, 'What do
you like about yourself?'

What did she like about herself? She went
to say something glib, like her hair, but then
he smiled, an unexpected and gently encouraging smile, and she heard herself say,
'I do keep trying…even when I don't want
to.'

Well, that probably made no sense to
him…but it made sense to her. After Dan
had split with her, some of her ex-colleagues,
awkward with the whole situation between
herself and Dan, had distanced themselves

from her. In the end she had decided to search for another job, the awkwardness with her colleagues and having to face Dan every day proving too stressful.

But she had picked herself up and got on with life. That had to count for something, didn't it?

To her amazement he smiled. Her heart danced to see his grin. 'I like determination in a person.'

Her belly flipped at the soft intimacy in his voice. 'I hope you're still saying that in four days' time… I really want to get to know you.' Pausing, she knew she should clarify what she meant by that for the sake of the listeners, but a charge, an intimacy, ran between them at her words.

He lifted an eyebrow. And her heart slammed to a stop, this almost playful, teasing side to him even more disarming than his usual reserved demeanour. 'Dinner with friends or dinner for two?'

'I guess dinner for two can be special… depending on who it's with, of course.'

Oh, God. She wasn't supposed to be flirting with him.

He considered her answer, a glint of what

possibly might be amusement in his eyes again. Whether he was laughing with her or at her was, of course, debatable.

'What do you fear the most?'

Being too scared to do the right thing to protect myself...like how I should have ended my relationship with Dan long before he left. How I should have ended all contact with my dad much earlier than I did, knowing his unpredictability, how he came in and out of my life to suit himself, was damaging me. It wasn't only my mum who time and time again fell for his apologies. I would ignore all the evidence of the past—how he would turn up on our doorstep after months of little or no contact— and instead cling to the hope that this time he would stay. That finally we would be a family, that the sparkle in Mum's eye would last for ever. She was unable to resist him. She would go through a ritual of pretending not to want anything to do with him, but even as a child I saw the chemistry between them that skewed my mum's judgement so terribly.

She had learned from her father that love was unreliable, commitment only a word, but her biggest fear was that she had inherited her mum's lack of judgement and ability to protect herself. She *had* to be tougher. Less emotional. She needed to move through life with a more cautious but less invested approach to relationships. She needed to wear relationships lightly—enjoy them but not get emotionally involved.

But there was no way she was admitting any of that to him. So instead she answered, 'The possibility of being forced to eat olive oil ice cream this weekend. Talking of which, I will be staying with you until Tuesday morning. What do you have planned for the weekend? Of course, we have Princess Gabriela's christening on Sunday, which I'm very much looking forward to. But am I going to experience Monrosa's nightlife again? Regular listeners will know I'm a huge fan of the local cocktail, Paradise City, which I got to try when I was here for Alice's wedding.'

'There isn't any nightlife where we're going.'

What on earth did he mean? There were numerous exclusive bars and clubs suitable for a royal close to the palace. 'Aren't we staying at the palace?'

'No. We're staying in my *finca*, San Jorbo.'

She tried not to look shocked. This wasn't how she saw the weekend panning out. Should she protest? But on what grounds? She was his guest. She had to fall in line with his plans. Even if it was away from the assurance of knowing Kara and Alice would be near by. 'Great, it will be wonderful to see more of Monrosa, and I have heard that the towns and villages in the north are stunning.' Flicking off the recording, she disconnected the microphones. 'So, your *finca*—what town is it close to...and will there be others staying there too?'

'There's a town on the opposite side of the harbour, and we'll be alone.'

She stopped packing her bag. 'How about your security team?'

'They patrol the area but don't worry, they won't disturb any of the interviews.'

That was not what she was worried about...and, though his expression was deadpan, she was certain he knew that. All alone for four days with him...what was she walking into? Would she somehow over-come just how unsettled he made her feel? Would she ever manage to get him to relax and have the spontaneous and free-flow-ing conversations that she wanted to give to the listeners? And what about the sparks of attraction between them…were they even real or just in her imagination…but if they were real, what on earth was going to hap-pen when they were all alone?

'If you'd prefer to stay in the palace, that can be arranged. We can talk again on Sun-day when I'm there for the christening. With today's interview and a longer one again on Sunday I'm sure there will be enough mate-rial for a podcast. In fact, you can send me your list of questions tomorrow and I can prepare in advance.'

She winced at the enthusiasm in his tone. She obviously wasn't the only one not relish-ing the prospect of four days together. She plastered on a smile. 'That's not how these podcasts work. I have to spend time with you.' She stopped and cringed. That sounded all wrong…it sounded as though she was contemplating a prison sentence rather than it being the part of her job she usually loved the most—having the privilege to peek into another person's life and really connect with them on a deep level. She was still in contact with all of her ex-interviewees. Somehow she got the feeling that that might not be the case with Ivo.

Even though she was standing, Ivo remained seated, studying her closely, which was only making her even more jittery than she already was.

'I know things have been tough for you. Stay in the palace. Spend some time with Alice and Kara.'

She zipped the bag closed, shame keeping her eyes averted from him. Oh, God, he obviously somehow knew about Dan's wedding. Did he pity her? The whole thing was embarrassing enough…and now she had the man who was nicknamed *The Machine* feeling sorry for her. 'Make your phone calls and I'll go and get myself a Paradise City in the nearest cocktail bar. Come find me when you're ready to leave. I'll treat you to a Friday night drink before we disappear into the wilderness.'

She walked away, knowing she was leaving one unimpressed prince behind her.

She knew she was being glib and perhaps even a little disrespectful, but the thought of four days alone with him was making her irritable…and a whole lot nervous. And when she was like that she needed noise and activity and as many distractions as she could find.

CHAPTER THREE

THE SUV THAT had trailed them all the way
from Monrosa city didn't follow them past
the heavy wooden gates and security lodge
that marked the entrance of Ivo's *finca*, San
Jorbo. But what did follow them were two
wildly yapping dogs, who only calmed when
Ivo drew his car to a stop and opened his
door. A little grey-haired terrier was the
first to jump in, but he was swiftly shunted
across the car and onto her lap by a much
larger dog who vaulted himself onto Ivo. She
patted the terrier gingerly, praying the short-
haired monster on Ivo's lap wouldn't decide
to spring across to say hello to her too.

Ivo murmured in low Spanish to the dogs,
stroking them both, his arm inadvertently
brushing against her chest in the process as
he stroked the terrier on her lap…and she
liked the press and warmth of his bicep a

little too much for her own good. She was tempted to leap out of the low-slung car. Give up her space to the two dogs, who were getting more of his attention than she had received for their entire forty-minute journey here. Okay, so maybe some of it was her own fault…she should have realised that she had misplaced her phone much earlier. They, and Ivo's security, who had been stationed behind his sports car in their SUV when they had left the cocktail bar, had had to turn around fifteen minutes into their journey north in order to search for her missing phone.

She had hoped their journey would be relaxed and an opportunity for them to get to know each other a little better, but he had answered her questions in his direct, unembellished way and that had been as far as their conversation had gone. The silence had been awkward and she had found herself running a one-sided stream of observations on the mountainous landscape they had passed through. But there were only so many times that you could ooh and aah over the spectacular views of the coast from the narrow mountain road, the towering pines and eucalyptus trees clinging to the craggy, sun-bleached terracotta earth or the narrow laneways of the whitewashed villages they had passed through, locals sitting on terraces in the evening sun, nodding their heads in respect as they spotted Ivo's convoy pass by. She had eventually run out of steam and, reluctantly giving in to his silence, she had wound down her window and allowed the scent of the mountain forests in. And after a while her whirling mind had stopped racing, the wind blowing against her hair, the ancient beauty of the landscape that looked as though it hadn't changed in thousands of years, and Ivo's assured and calm driving skills even on the endless hairpin turns allowing her the first moment of calm in a week she'd rather forget.

But now she was firmly back in the reality of knowing that she had a job to do. On his command both dogs hopped into the rear seat of the car, which was barely big enough to contain them both. Reaching for her phone, which she had eventually located under the cushion of a seat in the outdoor terrace of the bar, she asked, 'Is it okay if I record our arrival at the house? I always ask my interviewees to give me a guided tour of their house so that the listeners can get a sense of what their homes are like.'

Ivo eyed her phone wearily.

'A quick tour is all I need,' she added by way of encouragement.

His answer was a curt nod.

She opened the recording app and pressed play. 'So, we've now arrived at Ivo's *finca*. The surrounding countryside is mountainous and we are approaching the house along a steep driveway in a valley that runs down to the sea, terraces of olive trees on either side of the drive. And we got a surprise welcome when we entered Ivo's property—his two dogs came to say hello and are now excitedly sitting in the back seat of the car.' Turning, she pointed the phone at them, 'Say hello, doggies.' She giggled when both dogs barked in response. Ivo even cracked a smile.

'What are their names?'

'Paco and Lore.'

She laughed. 'Which came first, the business or the dogs?'

He drew the car to a stop at the side entrance of a traditional single-storey sandstone *finca*, topped with a terracotta roof. He looked back at the dogs, and despite his smile she could see worry in his eyes. 'Paco is twelve years old. I adopted him five years ago when I was living in Seville. And soon after I adopted Lore. I'm not sure of her exact age, somewhere around fifteen.'

He was worried about losing them. Something solid lodged in her throat as he climbed out of the car and pulled his seat forward, both dogs bounding out to receive even more vigorous rubs from him, Ivo's eyes twinkling in delight. His bond with his dogs transformed him...lightened him.

Stepping out of the car, she held her phone out, wanting to record the cicadas in full song, and wondered if she would manage to capture the crash of the waves on the shoreline below them for her listeners too.

'I'll show you to your room.'

Had he forgotten his promise to show her around? She doubted it. 'Are all of these olive trees yours? They seem to stretch on for ever.'

He nodded. 'There are over five hundred trees in total.'

'That's a lot of olives for one person to eat.'

He raised an eyebrow at her feigned innocence. 'My neighbouring farmers harvest them. I get some olive oil in return.'

'You don't keep it all for yourself?'

He shrugged. 'They do the work. Life is not easy for olive producers on the island, so they need as much support as they can get.'

Unable to help herself, she walked to a nearby tree, placing a hand against the warm, gnarled trunk. 'The earth here seems so parched, it's miraculous that they survive.'

'Some are over three hundred years old.'

Her attention caught by a group of different trees, she moved towards them. 'And you have lemon and fig trees too.' Wandering up some steps to a flat terrace, she added, 'And a vegetable garden. Do you have many staff working for you…a housekeeper, a gardener?' He had said they would be alone, but maybe he hadn't factored domestic staff into that equation.

Standing on the steps, the fading evening sun creating a long shadow of him on the dry earth, he answered with a hint of wariness, as though he didn't trust her reasons for asking the question, 'I have a housekeeper who comes in during the week. I take care of the garden myself.'

'Wow, really?' Her only attempt at gardening was a tomato plant on the windowsill of her apartment kitchen…she hadn't realised that too much watering wasn't a good thing. Moving further into the plot, she said, 'There are chillies, peppers, cucumbers, broad beans…' she reached across and from a vine plucked a glossy red tomato, adding, 'and an endless supply of tomatoes. And now I'm going to try one.' Biting into it, she sighed at the warm sweetness of the fruit before turning in Ivo's direction. 'Wow, that tastes amazing.'

He didn't smile. It was as though he was trying to figure her out.

And she hadn't ever thought of him as someone who would garden. 'I didn't think you'd have the time to garden…or the interest.'

His expression tightened for a moment before he gestured to the miles of coastline in either direction of the *finca*. 'I need to be self-sufficient here.'

Following him back along a path that ran around the house, she shielded her eyes when they arrived back at the entrance of the house, the westerly sun dipping lower and lower. In the far distance she could just about make out a cluster of houses set low in the mountainous coastline, boats in the harbour below the town. 'Is that the nearest town?'

'Yes. Laredo.'

'Wow. You really are isolated here.'

'Yes, and I like it that way.' His tone carried an impatience and, not waiting for a response, he opened the door to the *finca* that was painted in the same pale blue as the open shutters on the windows.

She rushed after him, conscious to keep their dialogue going for the sake of her listeners. Inside, the entrance hallway was cool in comparison to the intense heat out on the terrace, shafts of sunlight falling on the stone floors. 'How often do you stay here?'

'Four or five nights a week.'

Stopping to study the bright oil paintings hanging on the whitewashed walls, she asked, 'Why did you choose to live here in particular?' The *finca* was small. A fraction of the size of the palace apartments.

'It suits me perfectly—I live alone and

don't need or want a lot of living space. It's the outdoors that is important here.'

She followed as he walked away and into an open-plan kitchen and living room, embarrassed that her surprise at the *finca*'s size had shown through. Opening the terrace doors in front of a slightly faded yellow corner sofa, he stepped out onto a covered terrace, heavy with trailing vines, and pointed towards the Mediterranean. 'I bought San Jorbo for the views and access to the sea. I like to swim and sail.'

Joining him on a patch of grass beyond the covered terrace, she saw that a path ran from the terrace down to the sea. Standing on tiptoe, she could see golden sand at the bottom of the path. 'You have your own beach…that's incredible. And is that your boat tied up at the dock?'

Bending over to straighten a pot that had tiny buds poking up from the soil, he patted the earth gently before finding a more sheltered spot for it amongst a cluster of other growing pots that were bunched together along the length of the low garden wall. 'It's a ten-minute journey over to Laredo by boat but a thirty-minute drive. The car has to negotiate the mountain roads between here and Laredo.'

Crouching down, he began to pluck some weeds from the pots, the gentleness of his movements so at odds with his size. His shirt strained across his back, the muscles beneath working as he reached and pulled. The sun caught dark copper tones in his hair and the very odd temptation to rest her hand on his shoulder grew in her. His silence moved something in her. He was as remote as his home was. In past interviews, recording the tour of the house had been fun and insightful…but with Ivo it just felt all wrong. Moving to sit on the wall near to where he was crouched, she closed down the recording app and placed her phone on the wall. 'I think we've covered enough for today—we can record more tomorrow.'

He paused in his work and they stared at each other for long moments, her heart pounding. She wanted to know him, she wanted to reach him. And not for the sake of the podcasts. She swallowed, realising it was because she recognised a vulnerability in him beneath all of that solid silence that at first she had mistaken for uncompromising self-confidence.

'I was brought up in London. I've never been to anywhere so remote...' She paused, the fear that she was falling into the old trap of oversharing making her hesitate for a moment before she admitted, 'I reckon there would be way too much thinking time here for me.'

Moving to sit beside her, their backs to the sea, he leant forward, his arms resting on his thighs, tilting his head to meet her gaze before staring towards the *finca*. 'You don't have to stay here.'

His tone was gentle...as though he was freeing her of an obligation. She went to speak but before she could he added, his hand gesturing towards the *finca*, 'The accommodation is basic. I like it that way. But I accept it's not to everyone's taste.'

She studied the pale stone and blue shutters of the house, the gardens beyond that a little wild but utterly in keeping with the surroundings. It was all a far cry from the glamour of the royal palace but Ivo's *finca* had a soothing stillness that somehow was already seeping into her bones. 'You have a beautiful home. I would like to stay…if that's okay with you.'

'Because of the podcast?'

The easy and perhaps right thing would be to say yes. To not expose herself. In past podcasts she had revealed few details of her own personal life, not needing to, as her interviewees had all been forthright and comfortable with sharing their lives, but with Ivo she had to do things differently to reach him…and every instinct told her it had to be by being brutally honest about herself. Even if it flew in the face of her pledge to protect herself by being more closed. 'For the podcast…but for myself too. It might do me good. This week has been difficult…seeing the photos of my ex marrying…it has brought back memories I'd have preferred not to think about.'

She dropped her head, embarrassed at how exposed she felt to admit that to him, and waited for him to ask her for more details, but instead he said, 'I think you're right. Time here might help you. San Jorbo is a place of healing.'

Really? Ivo calling his home healing had to be up there as one of the most unexpected things she had ever heard. Yes, she had briefly glimpsed a softer, more compassionate side to him at the wedding...but she hadn't been certain if that had been a temporary glitch in his usual aloof demeanour. She studied him, but he would not meet her gaze. And she got the distinct impression that he was annoyed with himself for what he had just said. 'Does it heal you?'

He shrugged. 'I enjoy having time alone to think. There's too much noise in the world. Silence is underrated.'

She wished she could agree with him, but the thought of staying here all on her own for days on end would panic her. She didn't think she would cope. She'd desperately miss chatting to people. 'Do you know, I've just realised that I've never actually lived on my own?'

His eyebrows shot up. 'Never?'

Oh, crikey...he *really* was handsome. Of course, she had recognised it at Alice's wedding, had felt flustered around him in fact, but she had compartmentalised it away because she was with Dan. She jumped up from the wall and tried to gather herself as she bent to pat Paco and Lore, who were lying in the shade. 'I know that sounds strange, now that I say it…but I've always lived with people. I moved in with my ex while we were still at university. And when we separated I moved home for a while…but now I flat-share. My mum and I get on…but we drove each other crazy when I moved back in with her. She reckons I'm too messy.' She came to a stop. Ivo did not need to know about how perpetually disorganised she was. Time to get the conversation back to him. 'So, what do you do apart from gardening, swimming and sailing when you are here?'

Stretching his legs out in front of him, he asked, 'How long were you with your ex?'

'Ten years.'

She saw his wince. And wasn't surprised. It was how most people reacted. And what usually followed was pity. She braced herself for Ivo to say something similar.

'Are you still in love with him?'

Taken aback by the bluntness of his question and the intense way he was staring at her, she garbled out, 'I'm not still in love with him but I miss him being around… We were good friends.'

He stood, his broadness making him look

even taller than his six-foot-two height. He approached her, those grey eyes holding hers all the while. She swallowed.

'Friends don't hurt you the way he did.'

'Our relationship changed...that wasn't his fault.'

'And it wasn't yours.'

'I'm not saying that...'

'You deserved better, Toni. You didn't deserve him walking out on you after ten years without explanation...or the fact that he started dating someone else a week later. You didn't deserve him marrying in secret and not having the decency to tell you.'

She took a step back. 'How do you know all of that? Alice?'

He didn't answer except for the minute movement of one shoulder.

'No...then it had to be Kara.' She made an exasperated sound. 'Why did she tell you?' She held out her hand to stop him answering her question, even though he looked as though he had no intention of doing so. 'Don't tell me...so that you would do the podcast. I don't need your pity.'

He folded his arms. 'Good. Because you won't be getting it.'

How was she supposed to react to that? 'Yes…well… I'm glad to hear that.'

Cool as you like, he walked away, saying, 'I'll show you to your room. And then I'll prepare dinner while you go for a swim.'

She chased after him. 'I'll help you.'

He didn't respond and, picking up her suitcase in the hallway, he led her past a large study and then went into the next room along the corridor. He dropped her case by the double bed and turned to her. His expression was determined. 'Go for a swim.'

He studied the closing stock prices in New York and banged out an email to his North America team, inhaling deeply in a bid to concentrate and not give in to the temptation of staring out once again at Toni's black and silver bikini hanging from the branch of an olive tree. After her swim earlier she had entered the *finca* with a towel wrapped around her, her wet hair piled on top of her head. Stationed at the kitchen counter chopping peppers, he had almost taken off a finger, knowing that beneath the towel she was naked.

Paco, collapsed on the studio couch as

usual, Lore tucked into a pillow beside him, lifted his head and made a throaty growl. And then he heard footsteps in the hallway.

'Hi, there you are. I was wondering where you had got to.'

He stood.

She stayed in the doorway, her bare feet at odds with her above-the-knee turquoise pencil dress. She looked great. He hadn't dated in months. Was that why he constantly found himself staring at her? Over dinner he had watched her tussle with a bread roll and they had both ended up laughing as she had frantically tried to clean the table of the confetti of breadcrumbs she had created by pulling the roll apart a little too eagerly. Their shared laughter had eased some of the tension between them and they had spent the dinner with him answering her questions on Monrosa's history and geography. He had even ended up drawing her a rough map of the island, highlighting Monrosa's hidden secrets she should some time visit.

'Alice said to say hello.'

She had spent at least an hour on the phone…even though she had said she'd be five minutes when she had excused herself after dinner to call her mother and Alice.

'Alice and Luis are going to a party in the city tomorrow night—she asked if we'd like to join them.'

He had learnt years ago that being direct and shutting down any expectations head on was the most effective way to deal with other people's judgement. 'I don't like parties. But I can arrange for a car to take you.'

As though she thought he was joking she laughed and asked, 'Is that just an excuse not to have to go with me? I know I chat too much and ask way too many questions, it's my nervous tic—and habit from my former career as an associate producer—but I promise to try to stop.'

'Are you nervous of me?'

Her eyes widened. 'Kind of...' but then, any hint of jumpiness disappearing, a playful smile grew on her lips. 'You are pretty formidable...and I'm guessing that it's an image you like to maintain...the untouchable Machine.'

Now it was his turn to laugh. Since he had left the world of rowing, where bluntness was part and parcel of a winning attitude, he had lived in a world where people constantly deferred to him. 'I'll admit that in some areas of my life I can be really formidable...' He trailed off, grinning as Toni's eyes widened even further and heat crept into her cheeks.

'You still haven't answered my question. Why won't you come to the party?'

'Small talk bores me.'

She gave him a curious look but then her gaze moved over to the table behind him, settling on his painting equipment.

'You paint?'

All through his childhood it was only his mother who had encouraged his painting, his love for creating. Meanwhile his father had said that he should be outdoors, doing something worthwhile. And in school his rowing team had teased him over it, calling him Rembrandt. He had stopped painting then, hating the attention and how different he had felt from his teammates. Hating that no one seemed to understand the comfort it brought to him. No one knew he was painting again. 'I was just about to take the dogs for a walk.'

She went and lifted the sheet of rice paper he had been working on last night, studying the monochrome painting of the chilli. 'This is beautiful… Where did you learn to paint like this?'

'A few years ago I saw an exhibition of Chinese ink painting in New York and I decided to try it.'

'Can I have a go?'

Thrown by her enthusiasm, he hesitated. Painting was his escape, a fundamental and deeply personal part of his life that he didn't want to share with anyone. After his mother had died he had found solace in painting toy soldiers, the precision and concentration required quietening his mind, until his father had sent him away to boarding school. When he had returned home after his first term, all of his paints had been binned, his father telling him he was not allowed to spend time alone in his room any more.

'The ink can't be washed out.' He nodded towards her dress. 'It may damage your clothes.'

Smoothing her hand over the material of her dress, she rolled her eyes. 'I guess I should explain why I'm so formally dressed—I packed thinking I was staying in the palace. I didn't think to pack anything casual.' Lowering his painting to the table, she added quietly, 'I would really like to give painting a go… I'll be careful with the ink.'

He searched her eyes, trying to understand why she was so keen, but all he could find was a gentle eagerness. 'I'll go and find something for you to wear over your clothes.'

When he returned to the studio, she studied the embroidered logo on the white T-shirt he passed to her. 'You must be very proud to have represented your country in sport.'

He watched her slip on the T-shirt, smiled as it engulfed her, reaching almost as far as the hem of her skirt. 'It meant a lot to the people of Monrosa—we had never won an international medal before.'

He pulled an extra chair to the table. They both sat and he lifted out the paint caddy, brush stand and two fresh sheets of paper.

'Do you miss rowing?'

'Not particularly. The training and travelling were gruelling. My life was a constant round of aeroplanes, training camps and hotel rooms.'

Her gaze moved out beyond the open terrace doors of the studio, the outline of the olive trees and the mountains visible thanks to a full moon. 'It must have been strange shifting from that world to this.'

He patted the fine goat hair of a brush clean. 'I slotted in straight away. This way of life suits me much better.'

'Why didn't you change careers sooner?'

He had thought about it endless times during his rowing career, particularly after their first failed international bid. Frustrated by injuries, exhausted by the constant change, he had questioned his commitment to the sport but ultimately he had loved the focus, the silent bond with his team, the hypnotic pull of the oar on the water as the sun slowly rose in the east. 'I wanted to win gold.'

'For yourself?'

'And others.' He had wanted to prove to his father and his brothers that there was more to him than the silent younger brother who so clearly puzzled them.

Moving the brush stand towards her, he said, 'Explore the different brushes.' Pausing, he placed a small amount of ink onto the ink tray. 'Lightly dip your brush into the ink and create shapes on the paper.' He demonstrated some brushstrokes, using three different brushes, showing her how different pressure created shadows.

They worked in silence, the roll of the sea on the rocks below the *finca* and Paco's restless movements on the sofa the only sounds. He waited for her to speak but instead she focused on her brush strokes, swirling patterns filling her paper. He drew out another blank sheet of paper from the cupboard, fetched a sculpture of a tern from the bookshelf. With his hand hovering over the sculpture he talked to her about the flowing shapes of the bird, moving his hand over to the paper to illustrate how she could capture its shape by curving the lines and playing with the space between them.

Her nose wrinkled unhappily with her first line that was to capture the curve of the tern from its head down to its proud, elongated tail.

Placing his hand on hers, he said, 'Have confidence, hold the brush more freely, feel the curves, don't think…just feel.'

He guided her hand, creating the breast of the bird and then the beak.

And when he drew back, he got why she

looked away from him. Something unnerving was beating between them.

'Toni…'

She turned, those huge brown eyes troubled but also unable to hide the same spark of attraction that was in him.

'This is all…' He breathed deeply, hating how inarticulate he was.

She waited for him to speak but eventually said, 'Complicated… I know,' she dipped her head, her fingers running over the handmade rice paper, 'I'm here to do my job, but please know that when we're not recording the interview…everything is off the record. I hope you can trust me on that.'

He resisted the temptation to laugh and tell her that he hadn't truly trusted anyone for decades. Always attuned to other people's judgements, always knowing that when push came to shove people would always serve their own interests over his. He should call it a night on the painting and go and walk the dogs, but for reasons he didn't fully understand he wanted to turn the tables and see just how much Toni trusted him. He knew of some of her background, thanks to overhearing conversations between Kara and Alice, but would Toni share her past with him? 'You said that you used to be an associate producer, so why are you now doing podcasts?'

She grimaced at his question, running a hand over her cheek and back over her hair, which was tied back into a ponytail. 'When Dan broke it off with me, I left the production company we both worked for, as it was too awkward to stay working together. I became a freelancer working for a podcast advertising firm—I still work with them occasionally. Part of my job was researching podcast content and advising clients on their appropriateness as an advertising platform.' With a sigh she continued, 'Personally I wasn't in a good place. I felt overwhelmed by how my life had changed so utterly. But listening to podcasts, often when I went for long walks, really helped. I loved their immediacy… I'm naturally curious about people, not in a nosy way, but I love hearing their stories. Giving them a voice. There's so much power in sharing our stories. We can make the world a better place by connecting…' she held his gaze for long seconds '…in wanting to understand one another.' For a moment she paused and frowned before giving a disbelieving laugh. 'I say all that but sometimes I battle with the fact that I have a tendency to overshare. I'm a born chatterbox. My mum used to have to ask me to stop talking when I was a child. I was a nightmare at school. I know it has its downsides, oversharing, and believe it or not I'm trying not to be so open…but admittedly I'm not doing a particularly good job right now, telling you all of this.'

They stared at each other for long moments, the air in the room vanishing, his heart beating faster. It would be so easy to reach out and touch her hand, move even closer towards her. 'I'm sorry he hurt you.'

She nodded, her slow, grateful smile catching his heart. 'When Dan left me, it felt like I had been hit by a truck. I suppose, like any relationship, ours had changed over the years, but we were friends. We made each other laugh. One night after he had left me I couldn't sleep, so I went for a walk. I listened to a podcast given by a singer who spoke about her marriage ending and she said that she had been too scared to end the marriage herself, even though she knew it wasn't right for her.' She picked up one of the paintbrushes, idly drawing a circle onto the page, its circumference growing wider and wider. Not breaking her attention from the drawing, she added in a low voice, 'And I realised I had been too scared to even contemplate leaving Dan, never mind doing it... even though I knew deep down I wasn't truly happy.'

'Why were you scared?'

'It meant stepping into the unknown.' She put down the brush. 'I like to feel secure... the unknown scares me.'

Dio! She disarmed him. Her beauty, her forthrightness, the endless unnerving chemistry between them. He needed to be blunt... he had no idea what the next few days would bring, but he knew he had to make sure Toni knew exactly what she could expect from him. 'I'm not good at relationships. I like being independent, living on my own.'

Again she shrugged. 'Given that I don't think I'll ever have the courage to trust someone again, I'm trying to embrace independence too.' Her attempt at a smile did little to cover her vulnerability.

Without thinking he placed his arm

around her shoulders, pulling her towards him, and placed a kiss against her hair.

Just as quickly he pulled away. He stood up. What was he doing? He should be keeping all of this strictly professional...otherwise the boundaries between them would become a tangled mess. 'There will be fireworks in Laredo later—it's the *feria* week in the town. I need to walk Paco and Lore before the fireworks start.'

She twisted in her seat. 'I'll join you.'

He shook his head. Needing distance. 'Stay and paint.' He turned away from her disappointment, alarm bells that he was lowering his defences overriding every other desire in him...for her company, for her.

CHAPTER FOUR

SHAFTS OF LIGHT from the closed shutters fell across the bedroom. Outside came the frantic barking of dogs. Throwing back the bedcovers, Toni opened the terrace doors and flung open the shutters, squinting in the glare of the already hot morning sun. The stone of the terrace was warm under her bare feet. Following the barking, she ran down the path towards the beach. Were the dogs in trouble? She cursed as she stubbed her toe on a rock, hopping on one foot but still continuing her journey, unable to see what the crisis was, as wild and fragrant shrubs obscured her view of the beach.

She raced down and out onto the golden sand. Paco and Lore were scampering along the gently lapping waves, barking out to sea. Her gaze darted to the calm blue expanse. Was it Ivo? Was he okay? She called out to the dogs, who calmed for a few seconds before charging once again up and down the beach, their barks even louder than before. She followed them into the water, a hand shielding her eyes as she searched for him. Should she run and get her phone…even run to the security lodge and alert Ivo's staff? Was he even out there? Maybe he was still in bed? Maybe his dogs just barked at the sea for no particular reason. Her chest tightened. She knew she needed to stay calm, but she could feel her pores start to sweat, her heart race. What if Ivo really was in trouble? And then she saw a movement on the sea. An arm slicing into the water. And then another. A splash of feet. She backed away, collapsed down onto the sand further up the beach, relief wiping her out. She breathed in deeply, thrown by how panicked she had felt.

Both dogs quietened as Ivo swam closer to the beach, their tails swishing in anticipation as he stood and waded out of the sea. He was wearing dark green swimming trunks, his body a series of rock-hard lines of muscle emphasised by his dark golden skin. At the shoreline he paused and shook his head, a spiral of water arcing through the air, smoothed his tousled hair into order and then lifted a warning finger to both dogs, who instantly sat as though thoroughly chastised, but their wagging tails on the sand gave away their true feelings of glee to have their master back safely.

She stood as he approached, trying not to give away just how giddy she felt at his near nakedness, her fingers itching to follow the path of the water droplets slowly oozing down from the light dusting of hair on his chest, down over his pronounced six pack and disappearing into the band of the trunks that hung low on his narrow hips. Her pulse thundered in her ears. Did he have to be so disarmingly gorgeous? How was she supposed to breathe, never mind think straight when faced with so much testosterone?

He came to a stop a few feet away from her, his gaze briefly flicking down over her body. 'I'm sorry if they woke you.'

There was an intimacy to his voice that had her fiddling with the thin strap of her pyjama top and adjusting the legs of her shorts. 'I was worried something was the matter…' She trailed off, now embarrassed by her panic.

He shook his head, glancing back at the dogs. 'They go crazy like that sometimes,' then, pausing, he gave her the smallest of smiles, 'but thanks for being concerned.'

She grinned back, buoyed by the soft glimmer of laughter in his eyes.

An internal dialogue was screaming, *You are standing in front of a near-naked Prince Ivo—do you know how lucky you are? Make the most of every second of this. Memorise every detail of his body...memorise every smile, every look. You'll cherish these memories in the months and years ahead. An extraordinary weekend to look back on wistfully.*

'Can I interview you again this morning?'

Moving away, he grabbed a towel from the row of beach sunbeds behind them. They hadn't been there last night when she had come down to the beach for her swim. The door of the yellow wooden summer house perched against the cliff face was open, so she was guessing that Ivo had taken them out from there. 'I have to work—I spend Saturdays catching up on emails and paperwork.' He gestured to the sunbeds. 'I thought you might like to spend the day here on the beach. The summer house has a well-stocked kitchen. Help yourself to any drinks or snacks you might want.'

She got the distinct feeling work was just an excuse to avoid another interview. Her usual approach to interviews clearly wasn't going to work and instead she needed to adapt to Ivo's closed personality. 'How about we cut a deal—I won't interview you again until Monday if you agree to hanging out with me for the next two days?'

'Hang out?'

She laughed at the dubious way he said it. 'Yes, hang out. We can chill out here on the beach, go for a swim, chat, get to know one another. Sunbathe.'

As he walked towards her his eyes worked their way down her body and back up again. 'There are sun umbrellas in the summer house. Use them. Your skin is way too delicate for you to lie directly out in the sun.'

Something crazy stirred in her stomach at the heat in his voice. 'Well, I guess that's why sun cream was invented...and I like the heat. It's therapeutic.' She had no idea how to deal with the seductive chemistry that kept popping up between them...but, for now, light-hearted flirting instinctively seemed like the safest way to defuse its dangerous potential. 'I guess it's a good job that you'll be here to rub it on all those hard-to-reach spots.'

He held her gaze, a hint of a mischievous smile growing on his lips. 'If I'm going to forgo a day's work then it has to be for something worthwhile, not idling on a beach.' Shifting away, he moved towards the path back up to the *finca*.

She followed. 'Worthwhile...what do you mean?'

'I'll call the outdoor sports shop in Monrosa town—they can deliver everything you need within the hour. We can leave straight after to ensure we aren't hiking in the warmer hours of the day.'

Hiking! It was already baking hot. His towel slung over his shoulder, Ivo was powering up the path ahead of her, his long legs making short work of the incline. There was no way that she would be able to keep up with him. Her idea of a long walk was the ten minutes it took her to reach her nearest bus stop...this was going to be so embarrassing. She had to persuade him that it wasn't a good idea. She really should chase after him…and she would, but right now she just wanted another few seconds of watching his magnificent body at work, the pull of tight muscles across his upper back, the indent at the bottom of his spine, the hard round shape of his bottom… What would he be like in bed? Would he be gentle or demanding? Would she see a true glimpse of who he was beneath the closed veneer he showed to the world? Would the true man reveal himself to her?

A shriek cut through the air. Paco and Lore, who had been trailing close to his heels, bolted ahead, their tails between their legs.

Whipping around, he raced back to Toni, who was flapping her arms wildly and leaping in the air like a gazelle. 'Snake! A snake just slithered across the path. It went in there.'

He studied the dense undergrowth she was pointing back towards. 'Snakes play an important role in keeping our natural ecosystem thriving.'

Toni pushed past him, making a disgruntled sound. But then, coming to a halt, she twisted back to him, yanking off one of his old baseball caps. A trail of dirt smeared her cheek. 'You said the hike would be a short one—we've been walking hours.'

He checked his watch, holding back a grin. 'We've been walking less than an hour.'

'Uphill all the way, in the baking heat.'

Turning to survey the mountain forest below them, his beloved Mediterranean in the distance, he said, 'Yes, but look at the views. Wasn't the climb worth the effort?'

That earned him another heavy sigh. 'Yeah, they're fab.'

His lips twitched. So did hers. She tugged at the collar of her new T-shirt. 'This isn't helping—it's way too tight.'

Not in his eyes. Earlier when the outdoor store had delivered the hiking gear for her, she had tried it all on, grumbling that the sizing of the white polo shirt and khaki shorts were wrong, but he hadn't said anything, guessing that she didn't want to hear that he thought that the tight-fitting clothes revealed the soft curves of her body perfectly.

Reaching for the water bottle at the side of his rucksack, he offered it to her.

'I don't suppose it's a Paradise City in there?'

'Cocktails aren't recommended for hydration.'

She rolled her eyes and took a long sip of the water before saying, 'You do realise that we could be out having lunch in a restaurant with air-conditioning right now, or, even better still, lying on the beach.'

'Yes, but then you wouldn't be getting to see any of the hidden treasures of Monrosa you were so keen to hear about last night. Come on, we'd better go and find Paco and Lore—they ran off when you started screaming.'

Her eyes widened. 'Why didn't you say so before now?'

Before he could answer that it wasn't a problem, as he was certain they would find them further along the trail, she sprinted up the hill away from him. He caught up with her as she found the dogs lying in the shade of a giant pine.

Bending over, she patted them both. 'I didn't mean to frighten you.'

Dio! Those shorts were tight. He dragged his gaze away and stepped beyond her, gesturing that they should move on. They walked to the peak of the hill and then as the path dropped down and twisted inland he asked, 'Is there any other wildlife that terrifies you that I should know about? Where do you stand with lizards and spiders? The Monrosian Hairy-Back Spider thrives along this coastline.'

Her eyes widened but then, shaking her head, she said, 'You're teasing me, aren't you? Who knew that the Machine had such a sense of humour?'

He laughed. 'I reserve it for those who are close to me.'

She studied him for a moment. 'I guess I should be honoured in that case. Who are the people close to you? Who are your support network?'

For a while he pretended to concentrate on crossing the wooden bridge suspended over the river that flowed down to the coast. He was tempted to change the subject. But something inside of him wanted to tell her the blunt truth. He wanted to see how she would react. Would she distance herself from him, back away from the attraction between them? Would she get that he was never going to form close attachments to anyone? 'I prefer to fend for myself in life. I don't have or need a support network.'

Toni watched as Ivo walked ahead of her. What had just happened? One minute the mood between them had been light and teasing and now it was as though she had touched a raw nerve with him. Did he really need no support…was he really that self-contained?

She knew she should just accept what he said. Wasn't she trying to emulate his detachment, after all? But her curiosity was too great. Her need to understand him had her chase after him and without much thought she admitted, 'I admire your ability to be self-contained. Sometimes I wish I could be more like that.'

He glanced in her direction, clearly perplexed. Then he shrugged and gave a humourless laugh. 'You must be the first person who sees my preference to lead a private life as a positive thing.'

She laughed too, raising an eyebrow. 'Well, positive up to a certain point, of course, but I can see the merits of being self-reliant. Happy in your own skin, so to speak. In the past I have looked too much outside of myself for happiness—with Dan, in my social life, through work… I looked at all of those things for affirmation, but deep down I have struggled with truly believing in myself.' She paused, snapshots of memories from her life when she had felt overwhelmed by feelings of vulnerability looping through her brain. The times she had run home, only to find that her dad had disappeared once again. Her mother's withdrawal in the weeks that followed. The endless questions she asked herself as to whether there had been something she had done wrong to cause him to leave. The constant erosion of her confidence that had her cling to friendships and later Dan as though they were a lifeline of affirmation and safety. Her first year in university when everyone else had seemed so confident and she had just felt utterly lost. 'Sometimes I wish I was tougher, less thin-skinned, that I was someone who could brush off life easily. Someone like you, in fact.'

He came to a stop, his expression intense.

He shook his head. 'No. Don't wish to be anything but what you are.' He stepped back, ran a hand through his hair and grimaced. 'Look…in the past I struggled with accepting who I am. In my teenage years, I was always being compared to my brothers. I knew people wondered why I wasn't as gregarious as Luis, as charismatic and high-achieving as Edwin. But with time, I learnt that I had to accept who I am.' As he stepped back closer to her, his voice dropped a notch and his eyes held hers with a frank openness that had her heart turn over. 'Be true to who you are, Toni. Accept all of your qualities, use them to your advantage. My way of doing things…well, I accept that it's not for everyone. But it's right for me. I need privacy and isolation, the ability to focus… I guess that's why I'm an investment manager obsessed with hard facts and figures. You're a rising star in the podcast interview world for a reason and maybe that's tied up with what you call being thin-skinned, but I would call being empathetic.'

She laughed. 'A rising star—who told you that?'

He began to walk away. 'Kara…' Pausing, he turned and then added, 'Kara and I listened to all of your other podcasts.'

He had? She didn't know whether to be thrilled or worried. She caught up with him. 'You listened to them all? When?'

'Thursday night after I had agreed to take part in the interview—I thought I should find out what I was letting myself in for.'

She waited for him to say more, wanting to know what he thought of her work. She clinched her hands, her body tense with the need to hear his opinion on her work, until it dawned on her that silence was probably so natural and normal to Ivo that she would have to draw him out. She blew out a breath. 'So, what did you think of them?'

'The interviews? They're engaging. You're good at your job.'

'Do you really think so?'

He came to a stop. 'Well, what do you think? Do you think you do a good job?'

She winced. 'Sorry… I must sound pathetic.'

The most gorgeous smile played out on his lips. 'I wouldn't say that…' he tilted his head '…in fact, I would say that you have a passionate personality…you have an open heart and nature, which people obviously warm to. Don't knock yourself for being that way…accept it.' His gaze darkened. 'Accept your warmth, your openness…as I said before, be true to yourself.'

God almighty, did he have to stare at her so intensely, speak in such a low voice? It felt as if he was making love to her with his eyes and voice.

He tilted back her cap, his thumb rubbing against her cheek. 'By the way, you're looking a little grimy.'

Her heart somersaulted at the teasing in his voice, and for the briefest moment as his head dropped down she thought he was about to kiss her, but, as though catching himself, he straightened and instead led her along the path they had been climbing until it twisted to reveal a tiny village of white houses in the valley beneath them. A square stood at the centre of the village, several narrow alleyways that could just about accommodate a single car converging together at this heart of the village.

'This is our first stop—Almijara,' he explained.

Feeling light-headed from both the heat and the fact that she was certain that Ivo had been close to kissing her, she breathed out on a sigh, 'It's so beautiful.'

He turned and watched her, heat and laughter in his eyes. 'Like so many things around here.'

His mouth twitching, no doubt in response to her blushing so fiercely, he turned his attention back towards the village. 'A few years back Almijara was close to being deserted, but the remaining families came together and developed a co-operative.' He guided her down the track, pointing out the newly whitewashed houses that had been recently renovated in a bid to attract families back to the village.

The shade of the narrow alleyways was a welcome relief from the burning intensity of the sun. Pulling off her baseball cap, she slowed her pace, taking the time to admire the second-floor Juliet balconies at the front of the higgledy-piggledy assortment of houses, wondering just how ancient the cobblestones were. It was the utter silence that surprised her the most, and when they moved out into the square she asked, 'Why

did people leave such a beautiful village?'
She gestured to a now empty grocery store
and the blank menu board next to what once
must have been the village taverna.

'For a number of years the village was cut
off because of a major landslide. To reach
the outside world the villagers were forced
to travel down to the coast to take a boat to
get to the nearby towns. It was unworkable
for those with children, as there's no school
in the village. The road has now reopened
but the lack of employment opportunities lo-
cally has kept people away. The co-operative
is hoping to change that.'

She followed him when he led her down
a steep, narrow alleyway, her already exhausted legs protesting at the sharp decline,
and into a large building, its ancient and
huge double doors painted in green. Inside
he explained, 'The river we crossed earlier
flows down into Almijara and used to power
the mill that once was located in this building. Nowadays it's the headquarters of the
co-operative.'

'Ivo!'

A woman emerged from one of the rooms

off the entrance hallway and drew Ivo into a warm hug.

Turning, he said, 'Toni, this is Carmen, the instigator and now project manager for the co-operative.'

Smiling fondly at the immaculately groomed and elegantly dressed woman, he added, 'You should interview Carmen for one of your podcasts.' Turning back to Carmen, he explained why she was spending the weekend with him and Toni could see that Carmen instantly embraced the publicity opportunity participating in an interview would bring. Disarmed, she reluctantly followed Carmen when Ivo suggested that Carmen give her a tour of the mill. Did he not even think to mention any of this to her? But her misgivings were soon forgotten as Carmen took her on a whirlwind introduction to the other members of the co-operative. When Ivo had mentioned a co-operative she had envisaged craftspeople, when in fact the mill was home to an array of professionals—Irene, an architect, Alberto, an IT security expert, Salvador, a freelance graphic designer. She was blown away by their enthusiasm for the project to bring the village back to life and quickly realised that, while Carmen was the driving force behind the project, it was Ivo who was their financial backer.

And after half an hour in Carmen's company Toni could understand why Ivo had suggested that she interview the founder of the co-operative. Carmen's enthusiasm for the project, her tenacity in the face of many obstacles, her warmth and wit, her personal battle with breast cancer, which had been the catalyst for wanting to restore the place of her birth, were all truly inspiring.

Before they left the village to continue their hike, she and Carmen exchanged contact details, Toni excited at the prospect of coming back to the village to interview Carmen in the near future. And as they followed the road out of the village, down towards the coast, she glanced at Ivo. How would he react if she called to say that she was returning to Monrosa to interview Carmen? Would he be open to their meeting up, spending time together? Would she even want that?

'Carmen told me that you are the financial backer for the entire village rejuvenation project. I'm guessing it's a major investment, considering all of the building renovations and the broadband roll-out that it entailed. What was it particularly that made you want to support it?'

'We need to protect our villages. Up until fifty years ago Monrosa was a mainly rural country. If we lose our villages, and we have lost many here in the north of the island, then we will lose many traditions and ways of life.'

The sun was now at its height and, though mercifully her new hiking boots fitted perfectly, her top and shorts were clinging to her even more, thanks to the mounting heat of the day. She thought longingly of sinking her feet into soft sand…or, even better yet, the refreshing coolness of water. She eyed the sea below them. 'Can we go for a swim?'

He lifted an eyebrow. 'Did you pack a swimming costume?'

She hadn't thought about that. But there was no way she was giving in to his obvious teasing. 'No…but I can swim in my underwear…it's not against any law or royal protocol, is it?'

His brow furrowed as though he was seriously considering this. 'I don't think so.

We're a pretty liberal society. In fact, it's perfectly acceptable to swim in the nude as per the Freedom to Nudity convention Prince Ferdinand passed in the seventeenth century.'

She stifled a laugh, trying not to give away just how perturbed she was by his suggestion or even worse still at how keenly he seemed to be embracing the idea. Ivo may on the surface appear reserved but beneath it there was a whole load of testosterone.

And as they continued their hike she wondered at the façade Ivo presented to the world. Why did he allow so few people to see his humour, his empathy towards others? She turned and considered him, wondering just how easily he would erect those pillars of self-containment around himself with her, if she pushed him to reveal more about himself. Should she leave well alone? Not push to know him better? But she owed it to her listeners to dig a little deeper into his personality. 'For someone who is as self-contained as you are, the so-called *Machine*, you show a lot of kindness and empathy towards others.'

He shrugged but didn't answer.

'Carmen also told me about your financial support for the local olive growers. You seem very willing to give to others, whether that's the co-operative, your staff, local farmers…but you don't ever want anything back. Is that about controlling the situation, not making yourself vulnerable to anyone?'

Pulling his water bottle from his rucksack, he took a long swig. She waited for him to respond but instead he just continued to walk on in silence.

She waited and waited and waited for him to say something. And eventually she said with a sigh, 'You really are a man of few words.'

He turned and regarded her, his shrug not matching the weariness in his eyes. 'I was thinking.'

'About what?'

'What you just said, of course.'

'And…'

He gave another shrug. 'You could be right.'

She waited for him to say something more, but they continued walking in silence. And then despite herself she started laughing, and when he glanced at her she said, 'You really are impossible.' Why she was laughing she had no idea, but there was something about Ivo's ability to fall into silence, to seemingly just accept something and move on, that was deeply refreshing in comparison to the constant chatter that went on in her own head.

Directing Toni through a coded gate that took them back onto San Jorbo land, they followed a path down to a private beach. He smiled at Toni's surprised laughter when she spotted a picnic blanket spread out on the sand, a cooler box positioned in the shade, and a jet ski out on the water, their transport home later, all delivered by his staff earlier.

Dropping his rucksack onto the picnic blanket, he folded his arms and with a raised eyebrow nodded towards the gently lapping waves. 'So, do you still want to swim?'

Toni had been right when she had asked if he didn't look for anything from others. Life was so much easier when he kept people at arm's length. When he was in control of the relationship and could maintain a safe distance. But somehow Toni was getting under his skin. Her chatter, her sunny nature, her empathy, the chemistry between them were all deeply unsettling. He could fight her on the emotional front, keep her at a distance... but with each passing hour his physical resistance was fading.

Considering his question, Toni tilted her head. 'Only if you join me.'

Dio! How was he supposed to resist that teasing smile, the quiet suggestion in her eyes?

But there were things that needed to be said. 'You're still hurting... I don't want you to regret anything from this weekend.'

She raised her chin, pride shining in her eyes. 'What I want right now is to have some fun.'

'Define fun.'

With a laugh she gestured around her. 'Well, this is all a good start. Glorious sunshine, a beautiful beach,' pausing to study him, she added, 'and good company. I'm not looking for anything serious, I just want to chill out and enjoy myself.' Then, tossing her hat down onto the blanket, she lifted her T-shirt slightly, exposing the smooth, pale skin of her stomach, merriment dancing in her eyes. 'So are you going to join me?'

He waited for her to lift her T-shirt even further but instead she left it hovering with just an inch of skin showing, her teasing smile catching in his heart. *Dio!* The world felt like a better place when she smiled.

Unbuttoning his polo shirt, he tugged it off, smiling at how her eyes feasted on his chest and abs. Desire punched through him. He folded his arms, waiting for her to make the next move.

She eyed him as though trying to decide the best plan of action. And then in one smooth stroke she whipped off her top, revealing a green and white lace bra beneath.

His pulse thundered in his ears as he took in the swell of her generous breasts cupped in the lace, his mouth drying out when she unbuttoned her shorts to reveal matching underwear.

Again she lifted her chin but there was a shyness to her defiance this time. His heart swelled with tenderness. Yes, she was doing this for herself but there was a light in her eyes that said she was doing it for him too.

Walking to her, he smiled as his hands cupped her face. She smiled back, her brown eyes glittering with desire…and fun.

His life was so serious, so controlled. Toni's energy and spontaneity drove that home with a force that was startling. 'I need some fun in my life too,' he admitted.

Her eyes shone even brighter. 'Good.'

Lowering his head, their eyes teasing one another, his mouth found hers. Her lips were soft and warm. A long sigh travelled through his body before he pulled her against him, desire then nearly having him stumble backwards at how glorious her body felt pressed against his.

Her hands crept around his neck. He deepened the kiss, all thought abandoned to the sweet heat of her mouth.

She gave a sharp inhale when he touched the bottom of her spine, his fingers stroking the top of her panties.

Her body moved in a slow dance against his. Within minutes he was in danger of rushing things, of giving in to the temptation of lying her down on the sand and fully knowing her body.

Reluctantly he pulled away. His breath unsteady, he yanked off his own shorts and, taking her hand in his, led her to the water.

Breaking free, she challenged him to a race and when he caught up with her they kissed again, plunging beneath the water before they spluttered to the surface, laughing.

With her hair slicked back, her eyes glistening like the high sun reflecting off the sea, he kissed away every single drop of seawater on her face, her legs wrapping around his waist.

She gasped when his hand moved against the side of her breast, shuddered against him when his thumb flicked over her nipple.

He kissed her long and hard, her legs wrapping even tighter around him.

He couldn't get enough of her. There was something sweetly addictive about how she tasted and felt, the chemistry between them like a separate force.

Knowing he needed to slow things down, he guided her out of the water. Covering her with a towel, he patted her dry, drinking in her smiles, the soft wonder in her eyes, pushing away all the fears bubbling inside him as to the danger of this intense attraction.

They moved the picnic blanket into the shade and ate some food, but soon that was abandoned again to long kisses and gentle touches as they tentatively explored each other's bodies, the desire to rush things tempered by the slow, sensual seduction of wanting to do this right, even if it was only for a few stolen days.

CHAPTER FIVE

TONI WAVED THE tennis ball in the air. 'Come on, Paco, one more fetch.' But just like Lore, Paco ignored her and ambled away to carry out a sniffing inventory of the shoreline. With the dogs now bored of the fetch game and the light rapidly fading, she had no good excuse not to return to the *finca*. Apart from the fact that she was worried that she might very well make all the wrong advances on their master.

She couldn't stop thinking about Ivo... and everything his body was capable of. On the jet-ski ride back to the *finca* earlier she had buried her head in the gap between his shoulder blades, her cheek lying against his hard muscle, her insides melting at his heat, his musky scent. And over dinner she had been jumpy and awkward, hyper-aware of his every move, babbling in her nervousness, probably driving him crazy in the process.

She had sighed in relief when he had said that he needed to work in his office for a few hours, but afterwards had worried that it was just his way of getting away from her for a while. Was he regretting this afternoon? She hoped not. It had been wonderful and sensual…and yes, fun. She had to keep this light and unemotional…but when those silver eyes held hers, the regard and tenderness beneath the passion of his gaze could make it all too easy to fall for him.

Across the bay, yet another helicopter went to land on a property on the outskirts of Laredo. Yachts and speedboats had been arriving for the past hour too.

Following Paco and Lore, who were already heading back up to the *finca*, she knew that there was no way she was going to be able to spend the entire evening alone with Ivo. She needed to take a breather from what was happening between them and get some much-needed perspective.

She knocked on his office door but he was not there. Moving further along the corridor, following a hissing sound, she came to a stop at another doorway. Ivo was in the home gym on a rowing machine. Dressed in navy shorts and a T-shirt that clung to his damp body, he attacked each stroke with stern determination as though excising some internal demon.

She swallowed at the thick muscles of his thighs, the contraction of his biceps, the power and strength of his massive body. What would it be like to have him lie on top of her? She hadn't slept with a man since Dan. Was that why her hormones were raging? Was it simply by virtue of being in the prolonged presence of a young single male that was having her have sexual fantasies that were beyond anything she had ever contemplated before?

She had to stop this. She needed to get a grip. She breezed into the room and perched herself on the edge of the treadmill. 'I'm exhausted just looking at you.'

He faltered for a few seconds but, regaining his rhythm, grinned at her. 'Would you like some one-on-one tuition?'

See, this was what she couldn't deal with, when he surprisingly flirted so easily with her.

'There's a lot of activity over in Laredo,

with yachts and helicopters arriving at a property on the waterfront—what's going on?'

'The singer Federico has a villa in Laredo, and he throws a party every year on the night of the *feria* parade.'

'Federico! I had such a schoolgirl crush on him.'

Ivo frowned before coming to a stop in his rowing. 'He's a nice guy...it's a shame his plastic surgery went so bad though...he's almost unrecognisable.'

'You're kidding! He was perfect as he was—why on earth did he have surgery?' Pausing, she let out a disbelieving breath. 'You're winding me up again, aren't you?'

His eyes shone with amusement. 'When was the last time you saw him?'

'I've no idea. He disappeared from the music scene about ten years ago... How do you know him?'

'We sometimes meet in Laredo. It's a small place.'

'Have you been invited to his party?'

Placing the rowing handle in its holder, he unbuckled his feet, grabbed a towel and ran it over his face. 'Yes, but I have no interest in going.'

'Why not? It'll be fun. It'd be nice to get out and meet other people.'

He stood, giving an impatient shake of his head.

'Please, Ivo…just for an hour or two… what's the harm in going? It would be great to get out for a while…' She trailed off when he walked towards her. Reaching down, he pulled her to her feet, his eyes blazing down into hers. And then he was kissing her, pulling her against his damp body. Her senses went into immediate overload, his strength, the tang of fresh male sweat heady in its vitality, and instantly she was lost to everything but a hunger for him.

When he broke away from the kiss he kept one hand threaded through her hair, his other palm gently resting on her cheek. 'I want to spend time here…alone with you.' His voice was low and raspy. And then he was walking away, muttering that he needed to take a shower.

'Maybe that's why we should go,' she called out in frustration.

He turned and considered her for a moment, but with a shake of his head he gave her his answer, and left the room.

* * *

Scrubbing his scalp, Ivo turned the water flow up to maximum and let the pounding water drum into his skull. Unable to focus on work earlier, he had hoped an hour's rowing would ease his restlessness and it had worked until Toni had arrived at the gym. The sight of her perched on the side of the treadmill, her red wrap dress accentuating the gorgeous shape of her body, had all contributed to wrecking his attempts to try and get some perspective on what had happened on the beach earlier.

The chemistry between them, so raw and urgent, was unsettling in itself. But as they had lain together and kissed and touched and chatted and laughed, a dangerous connection had spun between them. A fondness even. Fondness…was that even the right word? It felt like an odd choice of word, but nothing else summed up the gentle teasing, the natural ease that was between them. An ironic ease, given that it troubled him so much.

In all of his previous relationships he had been able to maintain an emotional distance. None of his exes had challenged his status quo—he had managed to remain detached from them, had continued on with life in the way he wanted to pursue it. But Toni was different. He had a hunger for her, an uncontrollable need to touch her, to chat with her, tease her, which felt apart from his usual self-control and logic.

He needed to create distance between them. He needed to make it clear who he was and that he wasn't for changing.

Towelling himself dry, he pulled on chinos and a lightweight shirt. He found her out on the terrace staring towards the lights of Laredo. Dropping her feet from where she had propped them on the side of the outdoor coffee table, she sat up on the sofa and pulled out the earbuds attached to her phone.

He sat opposite her, his back to Laredo. 'I like my life. I don't need or want to go to parties.'

He expected questions and protests but instead she gave him silence. He arched his neck against the sudden burning need to talk. 'I have always been content on my own. It's other people who have difficulty in accepting that.'

She grimaced. 'I'm sorry…'

'It's frustrating having to justify the decisions you take, all of the time.'

'Is that why you prefer to be alone, because you feel you have to justify yourself to others?'

Why was he talking to her about any of this? What use could it serve? 'Yes…no… look, can you just accept that I am happy in my life? I work and enjoy life here in San Jorbo. I don't need anything else.'

She flinched at his words and he regretted the heat in his voice. But then, meeting his gaze she asked, 'What about your family? Don't you want to be with them?'

'We have a complex relationship. We were all sent to boarding school from a young age, so we aren't as close as other families are.'

'Do you wish things had been different?'

'I don't see the point in wishing for things that are already in the past,' he responded.

'I guess, but it's okay to admit that things have hurt you. We all have things in our past that we wish had been different or regret… at least, I do.'

Something caught in his throat at the gentleness of her tone. And without thinking he blurted out, 'I was alone with her when she fell.'

Dio! Why was he talking about this? He clenched his hands. This was not what he had planned. He should just make his excuses and leave.

But instead he sat in the silence between them and as much as he fought it, his eyes kept being drawn back to her steady, soft contemplation. 'My mother—we were out riding. I had gone ahead, and when I turned back her horse, Cassini, was charging towards me without her. I found her lying on the ground unconscious.' He closed his eyes. How was it possible that that memory still invoked the same horror now as it did all those years ago? 'I tried waking her, but she was unresponsive. I ran for help. I should have stayed. She shouldn't have died alone.'

He waited for her to justify his decisions that day, or even, as his father had done, tell him to stop thinking about it, that it didn't matter. That there was nothing he could have done. His father hadn't understood... Ivo knew that he wouldn't have been able to save her, but the thought that she had died without someone by her side destroyed him.

Had she known that she was alone? Had she felt abandoned? Had that been her last thought? Why was she dying alone with no one to hold her hand, to speak words of love?

Toni moved over and sat beside him. He waited for her to speak but instead she rested her hand on his and he breathed against the instinct to take his hand away. This was not who he was. He didn't discuss his past. The pull to clam up, to withdraw from her, gathered strength.

'Were you able to talk to your family about how you were feeling?'

He laughed at that. 'We operate a *the least said, the better* policy.'

'Do you miss her?'

A heavy weight pressed down on his chest. Her hand shifted to wrap over his completely, the light, feminine weight undoing him in how she was trying to comfort him. 'She understood me. She understood that by nature I'm private and often need time alone.' He shook his head. 'Not the best qualities when you're born into public life, I'll admit.'

'I reckon Luis makes up for you on that front.'

She was right. Despite himself he laughed, but the weight on his chest still felt like a heavy mass. 'True.' And then he heard himself admit, 'I found public life tolerable when I was younger...but after she died...' he trailed off, not sure how to explain it all. 'I didn't want to leave my bedroom. I spent hours building fantasy worlds with my toy soldiers. It drove my father crazy.'

She exhaled slowly, her eyes holding his. 'You had a major trauma. It was your way of coping.'

'I needed space, I needed to grieve in privacy, but instead I had to publicly grieve in front of the entire world. I couldn't cope with the crowds, the television cameras.'

Shifting forward in her seat, she turned so that she was looking at him directly. 'I'm sorry that you lost your mum and that you weren't able to grieve for her in the way that you needed to.' She grimaced, shaking her head. 'I wish I could say, do something more than just say that I'm sorry.' She paused and he saw tears glisten in her eyes. 'I had never thought about it before tonight but I know that with my mum, when...' she stopped, clearly struggling to speak '...when she dies

I'll want to be there for her, and I'm so sorry that didn't happen for you.'

He had no words. So he gathered her to him, laying her head against his chest, fighting back a heavy wave of emotion in his chest, her compassion, her understanding, overwhelming him.

And then came panic. The cool walls of logic and detachment he had erected around himself were melting in the warmth of her care. He couldn't allow himself to be vulnerable to anyone again. He didn't want heartache and disappointment, all of the conflict that came when you had to negotiate your way through relationships.

He pulled away from her and stood. Nodded in the direction of Laredo. 'Let's go to Federico's party.'

She considered him with a dazed expression. 'Why…what's changed?'

I can't do this. I can't grow close to you.

'You're right, it would be good to get out.'

On the road beneath the terraced gardens of Federico's villa, the feria parade marched from the harbour to the town centre, a statue of the local saint carried on a plinth leading the way. Following her were local girls dressed in flamboyant gowns, their dark hair smoothed into perfectly neat buns, proud men on horseback, fishermen pushing their boats on trailers, and a flotilla of cars, each packed with an impossible number of people, smiling and waving and shouting messages of good cheer to the watching spectators.

Toni bit back a smile when, at the baying of those in the procession, Federico, with false reluctance, stood on the terrace wall and began to serenade the crowd. The hairs on the back of her neck tingled as the crowd grew quiet, Federico's rich baritone voice filling the night air. He sang his most famous song and soon the entire party and the crowd below were clapping and singing along.

Toni beamed. This was exactly what she needed. A brilliant distraction away from everything Ivo was stirring in her. Federico's villa and gardens were jammed with exquisitely dressed guests, the noise levels from the chatter and music deafening. It was like an extreme version of any other party she had ever attended, more glamorous, noisier and spectacular in its excessiveness. Uniformed staff, who had an uncanny ability to anticipate her every need, were constantly topping up her champagne glass and the other guests were warm and welcoming. Federico, on learning that she was a friend of Alice's, had introduced her to Alice's new personal assistant, Carolina, who had taken her under her wing and had introduced her to a dizzying array of other guests. She was having an incredible night…she really was. She took a sip of champagne, stepping away from a group who had travelled from Madrid for the party to search the crowd. Ivo was standing up at the villa with another man, away from the bulk of the partygoers, who had crowded down to the parameter wall to watch the procession. Both men would occasionally glance towards the noise and activity but were preoccupied with whatever they were discussing.

She wanted to be with him. This party was amazing, everything she had thought she had wanted. But it wasn't working…no amount of noise and laughter and distraction could hide the fact that she was denying yet again her true feelings. She had done it all of the time when she had been with Dan, papering over the cracks in their relationship by being too busy in work and their social life to ever have to face up to the problems between them. And since he had left her she had been doing the same, always busy, busy, busy, never allowing herself to exist in silence, never allowing herself to truly admit and accept the loneliness inside of herself.

She knew she should stay and enjoy the party. Revel in the chatter and good company of others. Have a few more drinks. Forget about everything that made her feel incomplete. Avoid the temptation to connect with Ivo, to know him better. Ignore the pull inside of her to tell him who she truly was. She should be sensible and stay.

But instead she walked up the garden steps. Waited until Ivo saw her. Her heart thumped as his eyes met hers, a charge running between them. She waited while he excused himself and made his way to her. She breathed deeply at his staggering beauty, her fingers itching to touch the silkiness of his hair, the hard lines of his face, her body alive to the smooth, agile movement of his body that promised so much in bed.

When he reached her he tilted his head in question. The sudden blaring of horns on the road had her reach up so to be heard and whisper into his ear, 'Can we go home?'

The rib glided over the moonlit water, the sea air rushing against them a welcome break from the heat of the night. Toni had yet to explain why she had asked to leave and, given her silence, he wasn't expecting an answer anytime soon. He glanced in her direction. Her gaze met his, a heavy beat of chemistry playing out between them. His eyes drifted down over her red wrap dress, her hand grabbing hold of the material to cover thighs exposed by the wind. Her feet were bare, her high-heeled silver sandals discarded. The dress highlighted every delicious curve, the sweet valley between her breasts, the swell of her bottom. What would happen when they reached San Jorbo?

Steering the boat off the path he had been following, he headed instead towards the faint lights in a cove to the east of Laredo. In answer to Toni's quizzical look he said, 'Let's get a nightcap.'

Toni's laughter was an echoing twinkle

when the bar's ancient jetty rocked as they leapt onto it. The clifftop bar was only accessible by water and as usual only a dozen or so locals were gathered there. He introduced Toni to Antonio and Dolores, the owners, requesting that they make her a Paradise City, which neither had heard of, enjoying the scene that followed as Antonio, who hadn't altered the bar's offerings in decades, grew more incredulous when Toni listed the ingredients. In the end Toni opted for the simpler order of a beer, just like him, and when they carried them out onto the terrace she gave him an evil look, 'I'll get you back for that.'

He grinned. 'I'll look forward to it later.'

Her eyes widened and she darted for a free table overlooking the bay. Fairy lights were strung around the olive trees surrounding the terrace, candles flickering on each of the tables. From Antonio's ancient gramophone the music of a flamenco guitarist drifted to blend with the sound of the breaking waves beneath them.

He spoke briefly to the other customers on the terrace, discussing the olive crop with Lidia, his neighbour, enquiring after

Ignacio's wife, who was in hospital, before joining Toni.

Toni watched Dolores bustle out onto the terrace to sit with Lidia, the women's eyes immediately shifting to study them. 'Why do I get the feeling we're the hot topic of conversation?' she asked.

He shrugged, the full consequence of what he had done suddenly dawning on him. 'You're the first woman I have ever brought here with me.'

'You should have explained that I'm a journalist, that there's nothing more to it than that.'

Shifting back in his seat, he studied her, watched as she drew her hair back and twisted its long length into a rope, the beauty of her eyes and mouth richer now that her hair wasn't a distraction. 'But then I'd be lying, wouldn't I? Because there is more than that to our relationship.'

Toni frowned. 'Why *did* you bring me here?'

He had thought it was simply to buy time, to cool that heat and desire burning through him. He didn't want to rush them sleeping together. He wanted to be certain it was what she really wanted. But now he realised he had other motives too for bringing her here. 'For a nightcap, but also for you to see where I like to go when I do sometimes go out.' He gestured around the rustic bar, the low murmurs of the other customers, the lights of houses on the opposite side of the bay. 'This is me. This is what I enjoy.' He shrugged. 'Some might consider it boring. Unglamorous. But it's what makes me happy.'

Her head dropped to the side, her forehead puckering in thought. 'Do you think that I'm going to judge you?'

'It's not what most people want.'

Butterflies dancing in her stomach, Toni tried to gather her thoughts. He was opening up to her again. Earlier he had told her about his mother and now this…she should be pleased and she was…but she was also scared. Not only of messing up by saying something that would drive him back into silence, but also as to what it meant was between them. She wanted honesty and openness, but it would make everything between them more intense and significant. And even harder to say goodbye. But she did want to know him…and he, her. She wanted a true connection with him, no matter if it was for only a few days. 'Maybe most people don't know what they want. Maybe they haven't stopped and really thought about what makes them happy and simply follow what society tells us what being happy looks like. When I was with Dan, if I was asked at the time, I would have said that I was happy. I had a great career, money, a nice home and a relationship. But now I realise that it was what I wanted to believe rather than what was true. At the start I did love Dan…but that had ebbed away years before we split.' She swallowed again, thinking about how their love life had been practically non-existent.

'So why did you stay together?'

'Habit.' She glanced away and cringed. 'Plus a little pleading on my part.'

His eyebrow shifted up in question. She couldn't believe she was admitting this. She hadn't even told Alice, too embarrassed by her own neediness. 'Dan broached the idea of us splitting up a few times but I laughed off the suggestion.' She clasped her hands against her burning cheeks. 'Where was my dignity? I used to make a joke of it all by telling Dan that we were destined to grow old together. I couldn't face being alone. It terrified me.'

He shifted towards her and gently asked, 'Why?'

For the longest while she could only stare at the hollow in his throat, the patch of dark skin where his shirt was open, and below that the long line of pale buttons of his shirt, a desire for his warmth, his touch making her light-headed. And then, cringing again, she met his eyes and answered, her laugh empty even to herself, 'Because sometimes I long for security…to feel safe. It's not great…but at least I now recognise that I can be that way and hopefully can avoid falling into the trap of an unhealthy relationship again.'

'Why did you stop loving Dan?'

She wrinkled her nose. It had just happened. She hadn't put much thought into it. 'He's incredibly smart and driven…but horribly disorganised and forgetful. Even worse than me. And as he became more successful, he became more stressed out. We used to have horrible arguments. I'd try to get him to chill out over whatever was worrying him, because in truth I couldn't handle the tension, and he'd just get more stressed out. The worse the arguing became, the more we socialised to forget about it all.' She shook her head. 'I hate arguments.'

'Why?'

She arched her neck, the low sounds of the flamenco guitar sending a shiver up her spine despite the warmth of the night. 'I...' she swallowed, tried to laugh '... I told you that I'm thin-skinned and I wasn't joking. I hate the idea of arguing because I have a morbid fear of upsetting others, that they might think less of me or might not want me around any more.'

'Would you really want those people in your life though, if they couldn't respect your point of view?'

She rolled her head side to side, trying to find a better way to explain herself. 'I guess what I'm trying to say is that I like feeling safe in my relationships, whether that's with friends, family or romantically. My mum always struggled financially when I was growing up. She's an artist but would take on temporary jobs to tide us over. I never knew when she'd get home from work. I spent a lot of my evenings alone. I hated being on my own. I guess that's why I struggle to be alone now. In my teens I used to hang out at my friends' houses and when I met Dan at university we immediately moved in together. In hindsight I can see that I was desperate to be with someone, to not feel alone.'

'What about your dad?'

She rolled her eyes. 'Oh, he came and went. He was an artist too. My parents met at art college. He moved around a lot. He lived in Italy and then France. He used to visit us sometimes and even persuaded my mum several times to give their relationship a go again. But it never worked out. They used to argue over money...and the other women in his life. Sometimes I'd go to bed and the next morning he'd have disappeared again.'

'And do you see him now?'

'He died five years ago in France. We only found out when his then partner wrote to my mum from France a few weeks after his funeral.'

Ivo grimaced. 'I'm sorry.'

She shrugged. 'I would have gone to his

funeral if we had known. He wasn't a great dad…but he was *my* dad.'

For a moment Ivo dropped his head as though studying his clasped hands that were lying on the table before him. When he looked back up she was undone by the compassion in his eyes. 'Wanting security, to want to feel safe in your relationships, is understandable.'

She gave him a wry smile. 'Yes, but not when it's the only reason to stay in a relationship. Dan and I were together for ten years…it should have ended long before it did.' Wanting to divert the heat of the conversation away from herself, she asked, 'How about you—have you had many relationships?'

'Nothing that lasted more than a few months.' Gesturing to their empty glasses, he said, 'Let's go.'

As they made their way down to the beach, slowly negotiating the dark path, he took hold of her hand. Her heart swooned at its reassuring warmth, how it sealed the intense connection between them. Nearing the end of the path, he pulled her to a stop and stared at her for long moments. Her heart began to pound, the beauty of the moonlit beach adding to the sense of magic whirling in the air. He gave her a tender smile. 'You should be in a relationship.'

Her heart in her throat, she desperately waited for him to say more. But nothing came. Why did he say things like that and not follow it up with details and explanations? How could he so calmly and unemotionally make such a pronouncement while holding her hand, the memories of lying together on the beach today binding them together?

She pulled her hand away from his, her frustration with him spilling over. 'Why?'

And who with?

'With the right person you could find the security you want.'

'I thought you were against relationships?'

'For me...but I'm not blind to how happy being in a relationship can make others. My brothers, for example.'

She gritted her teeth. Trying to pretend that she was cool with this conversation. That it didn't feel as though he was stabbing her in the heart.

Toni, get a grip. You don't want a rela-

tionship now. And especially not with a man as complex and detached as Ivo. It would drive you crazy, never knowing exactly what he felt for you, what was going on in his mind. Why on earth would you want to be in a relationship with a man who has zero interest in being in one in the first place? Remember, this is about fun. Nothing more. A step on the road to discovering yourself and lightening your expectations of relationships. You cannot fall at the first hurdle by falling for the first guy you make out with.

'Maybe you're right…maybe not. I'm learning about myself all of the time right now. I want to learn to be happy on my own, before I consider a relationship again.' She backed away from him, heading towards the wooden jetty. 'Right now I'm finding myself and thankfully shedding some of my old insecurities.' She straightened her back, a sense of purpose and liberation taking hold. 'I want to be light-hearted, freer in my relationships.' She waited until he joined her on the rickety jetty, laughing as it moved under his weight, emboldened by her own words. 'I want to have fun. Pure and simple. With no expectations.' She paused and gave him an inviting smile full of flirtation. 'What do you think?'

He eyed her for a moment, but then glorious amusement and attraction brightened his dark gaze. He edged closer. 'If you're certain that's what you want.'

She nodded. And giggled when he drew her into his arms, the jetty bobbing beneath them as he kissed her, one arm holding her tight while the other lightly grazed against the side of her breast, her hip, her bottom. The dull ache at her core that was her constant companion when close to Ivo blew bright and fierce.

She sat close to him on the boat ride back to San Jorbo. Her legs were weak with longing when they climbed the path back up to the *finca*, her heart pounding in anticipation.

When they entered the *finca*, he shut the door behind him and they were enveloped in the near total darkness of the entrance hallway. She waited for him to switch on a light but he didn't move. She knew he was near by. She could sense the pull of his body, the powerful force of his personality. Every nerve in her body was drawn taut with anticipation.

He moved in front of her, those silver eyes shining down with heat and desire. His finger trailed over the fold in her dress, lightly touching the valley between her breasts. She couldn't quieten her loud inhale and he smiled in pleasure. With one tug he undid the bow at her waist holding the dress together. Now it was his turn to inhale sharply and her knees grew weak at the way his gaze devoured her red underwear.

His hand lightly trailed over her ribs and waist and she gasped when his mouth touched against her collarbone before moving down to her breasts. His tongue flicked over the material of her bra, catching against her nipple. She swayed backwards but his hands moved to her hips, steadying her. Kneeling, he ran butterfly kisses over her stomach.

She raked her hands through his hair, the intense heat in her core and restlessness in her pelvis forcing her to bite back pleas for him to hurry up.

She went with him when he led her to her bedroom. Pushing her dress to the floor, he kissed her until her head was swimming with need.

Lowering her to the bed, he opened the curtains and the terrace door beyond, allowing in the light of the moon and the crash of the sea.

He shrugged off his shirt and then his trousers, his assured, agile movements making her want him even more. Lying down on the bed beside her, he held her gaze while his hands slowly touched and stroked her. 'Are you certain you want this?'

She nodded, incapable of speech, the low sensuality of his voice stealing away her last semblances of control.

He kissed her tenderly and her body arched high off the mattress. She pulled him tighter, needing more heat and pressure. He deepened the kiss, his hand moving over her breasts, rubbing against her nipples.

Removing her bra, he kissed her breasts and she thought she would break apart at any moment. And then his hand was on her panties, lightly touching her, exploring.

She breathed out, 'Please, Ivo… I need you now.'

For long seconds he searched her eyes and then, with a smile that touched something deep in her heart, he removed her panties and then his own shorts.

Her heart was pounding when he lay on her, his weight the most wonderful thing she had ever felt. Her world shrank and shrank until all she was aware of was pressing her hips against his, a dreamlike other-world sensation in her head as she lost herself to the pleasure of his kiss, the exquisite tightness of him moving into her.

She cried out long and hard when she climaxed, clung to him when he soon followed. Lay in his arms afterwards, dumbstruck that anything could be so perfect.

CHAPTER SIX

'Ivo, I saw your note.' Her hair tied back in a high ponytail, the silver and black ties of her bikini top poking out from her T-shirt, Toni popped her sunglasses onto the top of her head and waded across the sand to him, her attention turning to the cooler box sitting on the low table between the two sunbeds. 'What's going on?'

He had woken early and, unsettled at how good it was to wake next to her, he had gone for a dawn swim. She smiled while she slept. Why did that get to him so much? He had to focus on what they had agreed. A few days of fun. Nothing complicated. Nothing that would threaten his world order.

'You said that you wanted to spend some time on the beach, so I decided we'd have breakfast and hang out here for the morning before we leave for Gabriela's christening.'

She folded her arms. 'I thought lying on the beach was your personal idea of hell.'

Walking to the cabin, he lifted two sun-bed mattresses out of the storage room and put them onto the loungers. 'It depends on who I get to hang out with.'

Placing a bright yellow umbrella between the sunbeds, he opened it up and gestured for her to sit down. He sat opposite her and dropped the cooler box to the sand. Opening it, he said, 'I hope you're hungry.'

Her eyes widened as he unpacked the food. A platter of pineapple and grapes, drizzled with mint from the garden, and a tray of freshly baked croissants. Removing a flask and two cocktail glasses from the box, he popped a handful of ice into each glass and then the contents of the flask. Passing a glass to Toni, he raised his in a toast. 'My version of Paradise City...virgin, of course, given the time of day that it is.'

Her eyes sparkling, she grinned widely, and his heart kicked at her delight. They touched glasses, amusement shining be-tween them, Toni's murmurs of pleasure when she tasted the drink a potent reminder of her sighs last night.

But then her forehead bunched. 'Why are you doing this?'

'I've realised that I've never actually spent time here on the beach. Which even to me seems crazy.' He raised a teasing eyebrow. 'It's my way of saying thank you for last night…and I guess I enjoy spending time with you.'

She dipped her head, almost shy for a moment, before she laughed and said, 'Even if I spend too much time talking?'

'I never said that you do.'

She rolled her eyes. 'Oh, please. At Luis and Alice's wedding your pained expression throughout the day whenever we chatted said enough.'

'You were pretty excitable.'

She picked up a grape and crunched down on it. 'I was nervous.'

He nodded. 'It was a very public role being bridesmaid.'

'There was that…' she shrugged '…but you unnerved me too.'

He did? 'Why?'

'You were so serious,' she said with a laugh and a shake of her head, 'and so handsome. I was a nervous wreck around you.

You do know that you have that effect on people?'

He grinned at the playfulness dancing in her eyes, at the heady flirtation dancing around them. 'It comes in useful sometimes,' he admitted. 'And now...do I still make you nervous?'

She considered his question with pretend seriousness, a smile tugging on her full lips. 'No... I think it's safe to say that I'm growing immune to you.'

'Really?' Shifting forward in his seat so that there were only a few inches between them, he touched a finger against her knee. 'How about when I touch you—are you immune to that?'

He heard her intake of breath but she gave a firm nod yes. 'One hundred per cent immune.'

He shifted his hand to her inner thigh, his pulse upping a notch at the soft warmth of her skin. 'And now?'

This time she breathed out raggedly, heat forming in her cheeks. 'I... Shouldn't we be having breakfast?'

Unfortunately she had a point. Reaching

into the cooler, he pulled out the tub of vanilla ice cream and placed it on the table.

'Ice cream for breakfast?'

He chuckled at her horror and, grabbing hold of the olive oil bottle, brandished it before her. 'But this isn't any ordinary ice cream…not when we add olive oil from the groves of San Jorbo.'

She made a gagging noise. 'You're on your own with this one.'

He drizzled some oil over the ice cream and scooped out a spoon's worth, reaching over to feed it to her. She backed away, grimacing.

He ate the scoop and then helped himself to another few spoons before asking, 'Don't you like ice cream?'

'I love ice cream, but not for breakfast and certainly not with olive oil.'

Lifting up the dark bottle of oil, he studied the San Jorbo label before fixing her with a stare. 'You can have a lot of fun with oil.'

Her eyes widened. 'In what way?'

'I might show you some time.'

Her mouth opened. She went to speak but stopped, her cheeks growing red. And then she laughed. 'There really is another side to the Machine, isn't there?'

He laughed too. 'It's rarely spotted, but you do seem to have the ability to reveal it.'

'Did you mind that you were called that? The Machine? How did it even come about?'

Pulling apart a croissant, he took a bite before answering. 'My school coach was the first to use it.' Tearing another chunk of the pastry off, he continued, 'In my final year, I made it on to the senior squad but he dropped me from the starting eight just before the racing season began.' Realising he was no longer in the mood to eat, he tossed the croissant away.

'And?'

He was tempted to give her a glib answer. To feign that he had taken it all on the chin. But once again, the attentiveness of her steady brown gaze, her keenness to understand him, had him admit, 'I was devastated. Being in the starting eight was everything to me. I had trained for years to get to that position and without any explanation he dropped me. For a few days I considered giving up but I decided to prove him wrong and began to train even harder. Midway through the season he gave me my position back.'

'Did you ask him why he dropped you in the first place?'

'No.'

'Why not?'

'I didn't see the point at the time, reckoning that he obviously had his reasons. With hindsight perhaps it was because I kept myself apart from the team to a certain extent. Perhaps he wanted me to prove just how committed I was to the team.' Rolling his shoulders, trying to ease a kink of tension at the base of his neck, he added, 'Once I was back on the starting eight he started calling me the Machine, and it stuck from there.'

'And did you mind being called that?'

He shook his head. It could have been so easy to have fallen into the trap of giving way to the bitter disappointment of being dropped by a coach he had idolised, but the experience had been a valuable lesson in digging deep and staying focused and determined. 'It was a useful reputation for intimidating the opposition...and for my own mind-set. Rowing is as much psychological tactics as it is physical.'

'And now in business?'

'Clients like it—they want an investment manager who runs on logic and not emotion.'

'How about your team at Pacolore?'

He gave a wry smile. She saw straight through to where his style came undone. 'Let's say that it's a work in progress… I try to remind myself to take time out to be supportive.'

'From what I saw on Friday, your staff hold you in very high regard.' She paused, frowning before she continued. 'Honesty and openness are the lifelines of any relationship—whether it's personal or professional. Maybe if Dan and I had been more honest with each other, the same with my dad, then I could have avoided so much upset. I used to pretend to everyone, including myself, that I was okay with my dad coming and going from my life. But maybe if I had been honest and said how much it hurt me, demanded more of him, then we could have had a better relationship.' Meeting his gaze, she added in a low voice, 'Sometimes the easiest option is to say nothing…but that doesn't make it right.'

After his mother's death he had tried to

talk to his father but his father hadn't wanted to listen and had shut him down immediately. What would have happened if he had insisted on being heard and had spoken about the awfulness, the guilt of it all?

And perhaps the same could be said for all of his relationships in the world of rowing. He had kept a deliberate distance from everyone, only trusting in himself, uncomfortable with the idea of asking for even a semblance of help and support. Would he have felt less isolated, less apart from his teammates if he had had the courage to openly talk about his race-day nerves and how they had sometimes paralysed him? Or spoken about his frustrations and fears with the shoulder injuries that had been a feature of his entire career. It might be too late to amend the past but he could be honest with Toni. 'When you're unsure you talk. I go silent instead.'

Her head tilted to the side, her eyes silently asking him to explain what he meant. He swallowed, the irony of the situation not lost on him. He fought against his natural inclination to clam up, doubts as to what he was admitting holding him hostage. He went to speak, stopped, tried again. 'At Luis's wedding…you completely stole my voice. I'm not usually that silent.'

She blinked, those huge, soulful brown eyes sucking him in. 'I did?'

'You looked incredible.'

'I was a red-eyed emotional mess.'

'Not to me.'

'Oh.'

He grinned at her surprise, her slow smile freeing what felt like years of silence and caution and wariness of others. 'I thought you should know.'

'Well, thank you for your honesty.'

He laughed at her teasing gravity. Lifting the olive oil bottle, he asked in a low voice, 'So, do you want me to show you some other ways this can be used?'

For crying out loud, it was hard enough to resist him when he was all serious and cranky, but his sexy grin and the memories of all his touches and kisses and whispers last night were playing havoc with her self-control.

What would Kara and Alice say about it all? Would they worry for her? Perhaps, but somehow she reckoned that they would both be delighted that she was enjoying life again. And what was the harm? Both she and Ivo knew this was a fleeting moment in both of their lives. Nothing more than chemistry and opportunity playing out.

Yes, she had felt a pang of disappointment when she had woken earlier to find him gone, but she refused to dwell on the significance of it. They didn't owe each other explanations and she wasn't going to over-analyse his every move. Wasn't this the new type of person she wanted to be—laid back, carefree, not given to overthinking life?

Standing, she lowered the umbrella and, tossing a bottle of sun cream to him, she asked, 'Can you rub this into my back?'

She pulled off her top and then her shorts. Her heart hammered in her chest as his heated silver gaze moved down over her body. She lay down on her front on the sunbed, twisting her head to watch him.

Above her the hot morning sun beat down on her exposed skin, but it was nothing in comparison to the heat licking her insides as he moved to kneel beside her sunbed.

She jerked when he flipped open the top

with his thumb, a devilish gleam in his eye. He squeezed a long trail of the white cream into his palm. Her eyelids closed involuntarily, a long, slow sigh moving through her body as the warm weight of his hand touched her collarbone, making circular movements down over her shoulder blades. She arched her back instinctively, pushing her groin into the thick cushion beneath her as his hand drifted down her spine, his other hand lifting up her bikini top to allow him to apply the cream there too.

She screwed her eyes shut even tighter, wishing he would say something to break the intense and ever-growing tension between them…wishing she could find something to say herself but knowing that if she opened her mouth a deep sexual purr would escape.

She pushed her hips even further into the bed when his hand moved down to the base of her spine, stifling a groan when he reached the scalloped edge of her bikini bottoms.

'Toni.'

Her whole body arched at his deep whisper and she opened her eyes, her heart fluttering at the playful desire in his eyes. His fingers danced over her lower back, skimming her bikini bottoms. And then a finger ran down over her thigh. 'I'll do your legs too...just to be safe.'

'It's okay, I can do it...' She trailed off, giving up any pretence that she'd rather do it herself. Who was she trying to kid?

His smile grew even darker, more devilish. He started at her ankles, his huge hands capturing both at the same time, performing some magical pressure. She bit down on her lip, thrown by how malleable she was in his hands, every inch of her self-restraint dissolving rapidly. Instead she felt an unburdened, delicious, innate hunger that made her body feel weightless except for the heavy pulse of desire in her very centre.

His hands worked their way up past the backs of her knees, over her thighs, and then his fingers moved to graze over the intimate space between her legs.

Unable to take much more, she flipped over, her cheeks blazing.

He blinked for a moment, their gazes clashing, hunger and desire obvious, neither of them trying to deny it.

He yanked off his polo shirt. She breathed in deeply, the glory of his broad, rock-hard chest and moulded abs setting off tiny fire-crackers of lust in her stomach. She grinned in approval, arching her back a fraction. She was rewarded with his gaze darkening even further.

He placed a finger at the base of her throat and very slowly and deliberately ran it down over her breastbone, into the valley between her breasts, her already hardened nipples bunching even tighter.

Down, down, down his finger travelled, skimming over her belly button until it reached the edge of her bikini.

He raised an eyebrow in question.

And her heart exploded in gratitude that once again he wanted to make sure that she was okay with every step of this. This wasn't dangerous...this was safe. Her throat tightened with emotion. And she nodded yes.

But his finger didn't move. Instead he lowered his mouth to hers and kissed her tenderly, his lips brushing over hers. The emotion in her throat tightened.

He pulled away, but his eyes remained

glued to hers as his hand moved down over the fabric of the bikini and her hips rose automatically, her legs shifting ever so slightly apart.

She closed her eyes as his feather-light touch left her light-headed and disorientated. She groaned when his lips moved to her throat, her hands threading through his hair, curling down to caress the warm, broad stretch of his seemingly never-ending shoulders.

'Your body is incredible...so soft, so sensual.'

She tried to respond to him but she was incapable of anything other than nodding. In those moments she believed that her body *was* incredible, given the conviction of his voice. He did this to her all the time—looked at her with such regard and tenderness that it emboldened her, made her feel seen and treasured.

Opening her eyes, her heart flipped at the intensity of his gaze, deeply moved by how utterly seriously he wanted to give her pleasure. She shifted upwards, found his mouth, dragging him down with her, her entire body igniting at the firm heat of his lips.

She may have initiated the kiss but he soon took over the lead, his lips parting hers, his tongue exploring her mouth. It was a deep, lusty kiss that had her body arch, her nipples tighten, her breasts feel heavy and generous.

She gasped into the kiss when his hand skimmed over her stomach and up over her breasts, his hand cupping the tight swell, her nipple pressing hard into the softness of his palm.

She arched once again, her hands running over the bunched muscles of his back, his biceps, and the powerful and tight muscles of his waist, her hunger for him even more intense now that she knew what was to come, thanks to last night.

Crying out when his thumb flicked against her nipple, he somehow flipped them over in one smooth movement so that he was lying on the sunbed and she was on top.

For a moment she grew still, dazed by the shift, dazed at the freedom of lying on top of him but not sure that she actually wanted the vulnerability that came with lying half-naked on top of him. But there was something deeply sensual about the way the breeze was kissing her skin and she shifted her legs to either side of his wide thighs, anchoring her knees into the mattress. She gazed down at him, her mouth involuntary opening when his hands moved from her waist down over her bottom. Her head reared back, her nipples scraping over the solidity of his chest.

She kissed him again, deep and unapologetic, the movement of his hips under hers telling her that he liked what she was doing.

Long shivers ran through her as his fingers trailed over her spine. He was finding sensitive spots in her body she'd never known even existed—the indents at the bottom of her spine, the point where her neck ran into her collarbone.

He pulled the string of her bikini top, whispering for her to sit up. And when she did, he eased himself up too. Inch by inch he lifted her bikini up, his eyes drinking in the shape of her breasts. He pulled her closer, his hands resting on her bottom, his mouth closing over her nipple. She shuddered long and hard, the sensation exquisite.

He pulled away, desire tightening his expression. And she saw it in him too—

bewilderment mixed in with demanding need. How could this be so powerful? What were they unleashing?

He eased down her top, reaching behind her to retie the strings.

Unable to move, she stared at him in shock. Was that it?

But, taking hold of her hips, he guided her until she lay beside him, pulling her into his arms so that her ear was pressed against his chest, his pounding heart pulsing against her skin. He stroked her hair and whispered gently, 'Later.'

CHAPTER SEVEN

THE DRINKS RECEPTION for the small group who had attended Gabriela's christening took place in the palace's garden room. Clusters of white roses, named in honour of her birth, adorned the room that overlooked Monrosa harbour.

Seated with his uncle Johan, Ivo tried to concentrate on his uncle's concerns over recent financial investments he had made, but his attention kept being drawn back to Toni, who was standing at the opposite side of the room, moving amongst the guests, introducing herself with ease, her cheerful demeanour, her natural enthusiasm, breaking down any resistance the other guests might have to a newcomer in their circle. Now that she was wearing a knee-length fitted pale pink dress, her hair held back with a tortoiseshell comb, it was hard to compute her elegance with the tousle-haired, sensual woman who had gazed down at him with such open hunger only a few hours ago. He didn't want this elegance, he wanted her raw and sensual. He wanted her naked and a bundle of sexual tension.

It had taken every ounce of his self-will to pull away from her on the beach. He had wanted to tear away those scant pieces of cloth and worship again her body that was so incredibly responsive. Her skin, her scent, the way her body uncoiled, her gasps, turned him on in a way he had never experienced before. She slotted against his body seamlessly, her femininity a perfect embodiment of everything that was amazing about life.

And that, right there, was exactly the reason why he had pulled away. He wasn't making sense any more…even to himself.

Moving to talk to Edwin and Kara, she glanced in his direction and frowned as though trying to figure something out. He looked away when she smiled at him, hating how much he wanted to be at her side. This was alien territory to him, to actively not want to be alone.

He breathed in deeply, rattling off some

statistics to Johan on world market movements and central bank predictions, while he watched Toni chat to Edwin, who had grown in stature and unadulterated happiness since Gabriela's arrival.

Kara, holding Gabriela, was chatting with Luis, who was cooing over his new niece, Kara giggling over whatever Luis was saying, Gabriela staring at her uncle, no doubt as charmed as every other girl who had ever met his brother.

Edwin and Luis were working closely together now. Edwin's second in command, Luis was also the chair of Monrosa's tourism sector, which played a vital role in the country's economy. He had always felt apart from his brothers, but now more so than ever, not only because of their close working relationship but also their mutual delight in their marriages.

He stayed where he was seated when Johan excused himself to go in search of his aunt, Princess Maria, his attention once again drawn back to Toni, who was laughing at something Luis was saying to her. He tore his eyes away, fighting the empty sensation opening up in his stomach. And then the hairs on the back of his neck stood up. Instinctively turning, he saw his father, who was seated by the palace's permanent elaborate display of orchids that had been his mother's passion. His father was staring towards him, nodding at what Alice was saying to him, no doubt something to do with the latest of the Monrosian history books they wrote together detailing the trials and tribulations of his ancestors, which were proving to be huge international hits, but Ivo could tell that his father's concentration was in fact on him.

What did he want? Why the staring? His father was changing. Retirement and the arrival of his first grandchild were softening him, and Ivo didn't know how to deal with it. He especially didn't know how to deal with his father's awkward enquiries on how Pacolore was doing. Only last month he had unexpectedly arrived at the *finca* and they had spent an uncomfortable hour in each other's company, the sovereign investment portfolio the only topic of conversation that they had been able to settle upon. His father had left with the disgruntled expression of someone who had not achieved what he had set out to do. Ivo wasn't a fool. He knew his father was trying to patch up their relationship. But how do you heal twenty years of silence?

His father stood and walked towards him. He stood too, darting a glance in Toni's direction, intending to go and speak to her as an excuse to avoid his father. But she too was coming towards him, holding Gabriela, a brilliant smile lighting up her face.

His father was moving closer. Ivo stepped towards Toni. 'We should be leaving.'

She shook her head, handing Gabriela to him. 'This little lady would like some time with you first.' Then, turning to his father, she smiled in welcome and went and sat on the chair opposite him, a deliberate move in order to let the chair next to him be free.

How did Ivo manage to look so comfortable holding Gabriela? Wasn't he scared of dropping her the way she was? And God only knew how she would cope if Gabriela started crying. She had zero experience with babies. In truth, they terrified her. During the christening ceremony Ivo had lifted his niece from her father's arms and had held and cosseted her like a pro, performing a little jiggle to quell her whimpers when she had grown restless. Ivo set himself apart from his family, his silence even more pronounced in their company. But could Gabriela help heal the silent distance between them?

Now Gabriela's hand curled around Ivo's finger and he smiled down at her, truly enchanted with his niece. He looked so gorgeous... The Machine taken down by a cooing baby.

She caught Ivo's father's eye and cringed at his speculative gaze. Oh, great, he had spotted her mooning over Ivo.

'I understand that you are interviewing Ivo.'

Other than when Ivo had introduced her earlier, when it was obvious that he didn't remember her from Luis and Alice's wedding, this was the first time Ivo's father had spoken to her.

'That's correct, Your Highness.'

His father lifted an eyebrow. 'Are you having much success?'

Ivo looked sharply at his father and then at her, his expression tensing.

'Yes, it's...' She bit back a smile. 'Ivo is surprising me in many, many ways.'

She resisted the temptation to laugh at Ivo's horrified expression and turned her attention back to his father. 'It's the most pleasurable and thought-provoking interview I have ever conducted and your son is an amazing man.'

His father looked from her to Ivo, his expression astonished but then fading to what almost looked like sadness. 'I'll look forward to listening to the interview in that case. Maybe I'll learn something.'

Ivo frowned. 'You'll listen to it?'

'Of course I will.'

Ivo worked his jaw, looked down at Gabriela, who was staring up at him with rapt attention, and said, 'We still have material to record.' He held his father's gaze for a long, steady beat. 'Given that the purpose of the podcast is to raise mental health awareness, it's my intention to speak about Mother and the impact her death had on me.'

The air around them seemed to evaporate, a tight tension replacing it.

'That's private family business.' Ivo went to say something but his father waved away his interjection. 'But… I understand why you would want to.' Looking down towards Gabriela, he added, 'It's time we dealt with some of the past.' Shifting his attention towards her, Ivo's father added, 'I may not have always taken the correct decisions when it came to family matters and my children possibly paid the price.'

With that Ivo's father stood and walked away from them.

Ivo stared after him, his expression furious.

And then he stared at her, his expression darkening even further. She had done nothing wrong. Why, then, did he look as though he'd happily lock her in the dungeons beneath the palace and throw away the key?

'Care to tell me what's eating you up?'

Ivo gritted his teeth and pushed even harder down on the accelerator. Minutes passed, words bubbling inside of him, some words years old, others more recent. He gripped the steering wheel tight, pulling the car around corners.

Everything was changing. And he didn't know how to react. He prided himself on being cool and detached, thinking things through logically and burying anything he didn't want to confront. But all of a sudden he was feeling emotions that weren't part of him. Mostly anger.

'Can you slow down, please?'

He inhaled a breath and, though he wanted to press the accelerator even harder he eased back. 'I wasn't driving fast.'

Even to his own ears he knew he was being unreasonable, but he felt an unnerving need to be defensive and cranky...and to push Toni away.

'Why don't you let me drive?'

He let out an exasperated breath. 'No.'

'You're obviously upset about something.'

'I'm *not* upset.' He swallowed hard, aiming to say no more, but Toni's hand as it came to rest on his seat beside his thigh, the solidarity of the gesture, made him realise that he was bone-tired of leading a life of silence, of constantly keeping his emotions in check.

'I'm an outsider. I'm an outsider in every part of my life.' He paused, his words taking him by surprise. And yet he could not manage to contain them. Instead they spilled out of him like blood gushing from a wound. 'It feels at times that I'm standing outside my own life and observing it from a distance. How can I be so detached, even from myself?'

He let out another angry breath, frustrated with himself. Why was he telling her all of this?

'Has it always felt that way?'

What was the point in this conversation—what could answering her question achieve? Her hand moved closer, the warmth of her fingers touching his thigh. In response, the need to explain himself shunted his default setting of silence right out of the picture. 'Before my mother died, I didn't feel that way...at least, I don't think so. It was such a long time ago. After she died I didn't know who to turn to, who to trust, and it felt safer to withdraw and rely only on myself.'

'You didn't feel safe with your father and brothers?'

'They had their own stuff to deal with.' How could he explain the suffocating guilt he had felt after his mother's death? Why he hadn't wanted to be a burden to anyone? How he had been terrified of crying in front of the thousands who had lined the streets for her funeral? Displays of such emotion would have horrified his family. And worse still he would have been letting his mother down by indulging in his own emotions instead of respectfully maintaining a dignified bearing.

'It must have been a very lonely time for you.'

He shrugged, a heavy weight forming in his chest, remembering the days when he couldn't bring himself to leave his bedroom, watching his family come and go from the palace, desperately wishing someone would come and sit with him. But instead his father would send an aide to try and persuade him out of his room.

'Maybe, given what your father said earlier, you can now work on your relationship with him.'

'Perhaps.'

'Why are you so afraid to talk, to express what you need and want from others?'

He was thrown not only by what she said, but also by the soft emotion in her voice, and his cranky side reared its head again. 'Maybe because I don't want to.'

She waited until he had negotiated around a group of cyclists before she replied, 'I get that you are an intensely private person, but you need some connections in life, safe connections. You need to learn to trust people, know that they won't intentionally hurt you.'

He flicked a glance in her direction. 'Can I trust you?'

She blinked at his question and he cursed silently at her disappointed expression. 'I'd have hoped you'd know the answer to that already, without needing to ask me...but yes, you can trust me.' She inhaled a long, deep breath. 'But it's with the key people in your life, your family, that you need to open up. I know it's not going to be easy and that there's a lot of complicated history there, but I saw it in you tonight... I know that you want to be a part of your family. Maybe you're all in the right emotional place now for things to change.'

They were approaching the gates to San Jorbo. His anger had now turned to frustration. 'I wouldn't even know where to start.'

Not waiting to exchange some words with the security team at the gate as he usually would do, he drove straight through.

Toni twisted in her seat so that she was looking directly at him. 'Spend time with them. Invite your father here. Visit Gabriela. You're so natural and comfortable with her. A new generation can mean a new start for you all. Things can change, people can change.'

'Even me?'

'If you want to, you can. I guess it's down to what you actually want in life. Do you want to be part of your family and all of the positives and negatives that come with that? Or are you happier being alone, reliant only on yourself?'

He glanced at her and asked, 'Couldn't I be asking you the same questions?'

She shrugged. 'I have my mum and my friends.'

Pulling the car to a stop at the *finca*, he asked, 'And that's enough for you?'

'For now, yes, it is.' Reaching down to pick up her handbag from the footwell, she grimaced and on a sigh said, 'Can I be frank, just so that we are both straight on all of this?' She waved a hand to emphasise she was talking about what was going on between them. 'Even if I was looking to be in a relationship, you would be the last person I would want to date. Yes, you have a long list of incredible attributes—you're hot, successful, intelligent, et cetera, et cetera... But you're too complicated, too deep for me. You'd drive me nuts with your silences. I need someone who's upfront, who wears his heart on his sleeve. I'd be an emotional mess around you, I'd never know what you were really thinking, and quite frankly you'd exhaust me.'

How was he supposed to respond? Should he be pleased, insulted, relieved? Instead he went with puzzled. 'Why are you telling me this?'

'So that we both know where we stand.'

'Stand?'

'With us sleeping together... Why did you pull away down at the beach earlier?'

Irritated that she was so easily dismissing him as nothing more than a passing fling, he answered, 'Based on what happened last night, I wasn't sure we'd make Gabriela's christening in time if we continued...but I'm happy to make amends now.'

Oh, crikey. What had she started? Ivo looked seriously hacked off...and ready to pounce.

She leapt out of the car, her heart hammering. She bolted for the front door and had to wait for Ivo to unfurl himself from the car, stretch as though he had all the time in the world and eventually saunter towards her, his expression giving zero away.

Her heart was now a loud drum in her chest, her breathing so shallow she was growing increasingly light-headed.

He came to a stop before her and considered her. She tried to keep up her pretence of nonchalance but with her head thrown back to meet his intense silver gaze, her body alive to every perfect detail of his formidable body, his silence truly unnerving, she had the ridiculous urge to run.

The next thing she knew, she was lying firefighter's-lift-style on his shoulder, and he was carrying her down the path towards the beach, jettisoning her sandals in the process. 'What are you doing?'

'I think we could both do with cooling off.'

Down at the beach he carried her to the waterfront, where he dropped her onto the golden sand. Without a word he twisted her around, to face the lights of Laredo, the thrum of far-off music and the break of waves the only sounds. He drew down the zip of her dress. She gasped as he twisted her hair away to kiss and caress her neck, his hands slowly running the length of her spine.

He pushed her dress down to the waist, his hand circling over her stomach, hugging her to his body, while his mouth continued its tender assault.

She arched into him as his hands captured her breasts, his thumbs skimming over the lace edges of her bra. His mouth moved to her earlobe, gently biting as he lowered her dress to the sand.

She inhaled a shaky breath. 'Will we be seen?'

He gave a teasing chuckle. 'It's much too dark. Are you having second thoughts?'

She gasped when his teeth bit down on her earlobe again, an erotic thrill almost cutting her in two. He didn't wait for her to answer but instead turned her around to face him, unbuttoning his shirt, flinging it to the ground, his shoes and trousers soon following. His white trunks were moulded to his body like a second skin.

He dropped to his knees. She stumbled backwards but he grabbed her by the hips and eased her back towards him, his lips touching her belly. He moved across her skin with a painful, reverential slowness, her heart giving way to a tenderness, a wash of affection overwhelming her. He eased the band of her panties down an inch, his lips grazing over her hips.

She dropped to her knees and her hands roamed over the warm solidness of his chest, down over the steel strength of his stomach.

She parted her lips, wanting his lips on hers. Wanting him to take the lead. His hands cradled her head and his mouth found hers, the kiss light and teasing, his teeth nipping against her bottom lip, building up the tension pitch perfectly.

On her moan he gave her what she wanted. A full-on, deep and penetrating kiss, his mouth controlling hers, the pressure and passion a prequel to what was to come.

When he pulled away, breathing deeply, he stood, pulling her up too, his gaze raking over her body. 'Strip for me.'

She hesitated but his passion, his long, appreciative gaze on her breasts, on her hips, had her reach around and unclip her bra. She edged the straps over her shoulders, drew the fabric down inch by inch, her nipples hardening at the night air and Ivo's rumbling exhale of approval.

He cupped her breast in his hand, desire throbbing through his body at its firmness. His thumb passed over the tight bud of her nipple, smiling as she gasped.

He wanted to take her now. Push her down onto the sand, whip off her panties, which he hadn't given her the chance to remove, blown away by the sight of her gorgeous breasts. He had never desired someone so wholly.

'Are you okay with all of this?'

She pulled back. 'Why…aren't you?'

'I want to make sure that you are happy to continue.'

She let out a shaky laugh. 'I never thought I'd say this to you, but can we stop talking?'

He lowered his head with a chuckle, drew her breast into his mouth and sucked, the clasp of her hands on his head, her gasps for air confirming that the carnal pulses of pleasure pounding through him in tasting her, in having her nipple pressed against the tip of his tongue, weren't one-sided. He sucked deeper, a ravenous desire that was different to anything he had ever experienced making him lost to everything but the wonder of worshipping her body.

But after a while he reluctantly broke away, wanting her to know him, wanting her to know that all of this was not the norm for him...that this *was* different. Struggling to breathe, he panted out against her skin as he trailed kisses over her collarbone, 'I've always held a fantasy of having sex on this beach, but up until now I hadn't met someone I actually wanted to do it with.'

She gave a soft laugh. 'Should I take that as a compliment?'

'Yes, you should.' He paused, trying to find the right words for what he was trying to express. 'This is different for me...this is not the norm. I want you to know that.'

Dio! Did any of that make sense?

Clearly not, given her puzzled silence. He drew in a breath. 'With you...the need to be with you is different...it's real and raw and essential.' Pausing, he added, 'I hope this is making sense to you.'

Nodding as though it made perfect sense, she whispered, 'It does.'

His heart turned over and he kissed her again, this time with all of the tenderness and care he could muster.

And then he stood and led her into the sea, keeping hold of her hand as they waded through the tepid water until it was at his chest level. Wrapping her legs around his waist, he kissed her, the taste of her mouth and the salty water mingling, her breasts pressed against his chest. He deepened the kiss and she squirmed against his stomach, tightening her legs around his waist.

Still kissing her, he eased her legs down, his hands caressing her bottom, moving between her legs. She bucked hard against his fingers, groaning into his mouth. She pulled away, dragging him to shallower water, and once there she kissed him hard and swiftly before her hands edged down to his briefs.

He kissed her again, needing the warmth of her mouth, the sweet taste of her skin, every inch of him wanting her. His hand went to her hips, pushing down her panties, removing them, before he pulled her back against him, lifting her off her feet so that his arousal pushed into the hard bone of her pelvis, both of them rocking in unison, desperate for release as they exchanged brief, tempestuous kisses, both of them too short of breath, too desperate for anything longer.

'I should take you to the *finca*.'

She shook her head. 'No, I want to be your fantasy. I want to do it here…where it's raw and real…and beautiful.'

On a groan he left her for a few seconds while he found protection in his wallet and sheathed himself. Back in the water he carried her out into deeper water. She gasped when he pushed forward, her head falling against his shoulder when he eased all his length into her. Her body countered his movements, her kisses ever more passionate and desperate. He clasped her bottom, lost to the push of her nipples against his skin, their soft femininity, the endless curves of her entire body.

Her movements grew ever more frantic, driving him down a narrow tunnel of bittersweet hunger for fulfilment, but he clung to the desire to stay at this edge for ever.

She pulled back, her eyes glazed, her lips parting. She made a tiny noise.

Dio! She was beautiful.

His climax edged ever closer.

She let out another sound. One of pure wonder. And then, her head tipping backwards, her back arching, her hair cascading down into the water, she found release. Her sounds, the rhythm of her body bringing him to a long and hard climax, his body convulsed into the sweetest pleasure he had ever experienced.

CHAPTER EIGHT

SHE WOKE WITH her legs entangled in his. It should seem strange to wake in his bedroom but it just felt right. Just as it felt right to turn and find him staring at her and to return his grin.

He touched the whorl of her ear, his movement as considerate and thoughtful as his lovemaking had been throughout the night... well after what had happened down at the beach. Had they really done that? It had been wild and unpredictable. But in its aftermath they had returned to the *finca*, showered and made love in his bed, time and time again.

'You have sand in your ear.'

His voice was soft and groggy with sleep, his hair tousled.

She was flying too close to the sun. But so what? It would all be over in twenty-four hours. She wasn't going to overthink any of this. Instead she was going to stubbornly remain in this cocoon of pleasure.

She pushed him onto his back, lying on top of him, delight coursing through her at his groan when she nuzzled his neck, inhaling his rich, musky scent that spoke of exertion and freshly laundered cotton.

His hands explored her back with long caresses that instantly turned her to liquid. 'Your hands are incredible.' She lifted her head, her eyes rolling as she gave a tiny, carnal groan. 'If you ever need to give up your day job you'd make a wonderful masseuse.'

Pulling her down so that their mouths touched, he nibbled her lips, muttering, 'Your body is one sensitive point after another... I'll never get enough of you.'

She deepened their kiss, her heart jolting at his words. She knew not to pay too much heed to them—things were said and felt in the heat of lovemaking that bore no relation to life outside of the dream world woven within the confines of a bedroom.

Yes, their lovemaking was more than just physical—even she would admit that there was an emotional joining happening between them—but that didn't alter the fact that neither of them was looking for anything more than a transitory space of simply being together.

She moved down his body, her lips touching the hard landscape of his chest, the ache inside her intensifying as her tongue tasted the saltiness of his skin, his need pressing into her belly.

But before she could go any further he reached down and pulled her upwards, flipping her over in the process. Eyes aflame, he moved on top of her, his head dipping to her breast, his fingers moving between her legs, softly exploring.

'Are you ready?'

She nodded, hot, dizzying desire stripping away her ability to speak. Her hips were moving restlessly, needing him, the heat in his eyes burning her up.

And then he moved into her.

Their gazes holding one another's, they stared and stared into each other's eyes, a silent message of connection, of regard, of care, beating out between them.

And when his movements quickened she lifted her hips higher to meet him, and they fell apart together, the intensity, the intimacy of sharing such a powerful and elemental moment almost breaking her in two.

They sat on the sofa in the living room to record their last interview, the terrace doors open, the warm midday heat flowing in on a breeze.

She was desperately trying not to show it but she was nervous. There was a gentleness, an understanding between them that she didn't want to destroy by some ill-judged question on her part, or Ivo reverting to his usual guarded self.

She adjusted the cuff of her shorts—Ivo had said he would take her hiking to visit the most westerly point of the island after their interview—and asked, 'I want to talk about your rowing career, being royal and family life—is that okay?'

He nodded but the tension lines at the corners of his eyes tightened. She wasn't the only apprehensive one.

'You're uncomfortable with this interview, aren't you?'

He shrugged in answer to her question.

She needed this interview. There wasn't enough material from their other interviews for an hour-long broadcast, and what was there didn't give a real insight into Ivo. But could she really make demands on him because of her professional needs…? Somehow none of this felt right any more. She swallowed, wondering if she had served anyone right this weekend. Meeting his gaze, she admitted, 'I'm struggling with this… I need more content but I don't want to put you in a position you're uncomfortable with. Because of everything that has happened between us on a personal level, I don't have the professional distance I should have.' She stopped trying to figure out exactly what she was trying to say and, taking a deep breath, added, 'I want this interview to serve you well. Of course I want it to be insightful and helpful to listeners, but I also want it to represent who you really are, while respecting your privacy.'

'Why?'

It was such a good question…why, then, was she struggling so much to answer it? She bit her lip trying to put into words the twisting emotion in her heart. 'I've grown to like and respect you… I guess I'm struggling here with balancing how much access you have given me on a personal level to your life and what you want to divulge to the listeners. I don't want to be overly intrusive in my questioning.'

He considered her for the longest time, seriously at first but then a smile lifting the corners of his mouth. 'Thank you.'

She waited for him to say something more, her heart kicking wildly at the quiet pleasure in his expression, the warmth glistening in his eyes. Somehow her inarticulateness had got through to him. He understood this interview was a delicate balancing act in preserving what was between them.

She pushed away the thought that all her words were motivated by more than just doing right by him in the interview...that she was trying to maintain something between them that could last longer than this weekend alone.

Ivo's smile widened even further and once again the fondness between them morphed into heat and desire that danced between them wickedly.

With an exasperated exhale Ivo nodded at the recording equipment. 'Let's get this over

and done with before we get sidetracked...
again.'

Several times this morning they had attempted to get up, but every time one of them stood, the other would drag them back to bed. And when she had gone for a shower, Ivo had followed her in under the hot spray. And later, when attempting to dress, she had got as far as pulling on her underwear before Ivo had pulled it off again, ignoring her giggles and protests...making love to her against the door of his dressing room.

With a shaky hand she pressed 'record', looking at the questions she had written down over breakfast as Ivo had caught up with his emails. The easy silence between them had made her heart quicken and she had tried to ignore the temptation of daydreaming about long, lazy weekends alone with him in the future.

Now she said, 'You attended two international championships and were favourite to win gold at both. But, while you won gold in your second bid, at the first you famously finished fourth. How did you cope with that, especially the well-publicised media criticism?'

Ivo arched his neck, grimacing before he answered, 'Our performance at the first championships was crushing. As a team we didn't perform to the best of our abilities and we knew we had let all of Monrosa down. We had known that there were special screenings of the race being staged across the island and were inundated with messages of goodwill. Disappointing our supporters was the worst part. For a few weeks after the race I considered quitting the sport. The effort and hours involved in training at that level are gruelling, but I also questioned my ability on the water.'

'But you were considered the lynchpin of the team—what did the rest of them say about you potentially leaving?'

He shrugged. 'We all went our separate ways immediately after the race. None of us was in the mood to talk. The others wanted to be with their wives and partners.'

'Are you saying that you didn't talk to them about how you were feeling?'

'No.'

Taken aback, she paused, shocked but also upset at the extent to which Ivo had isolated himself. She couldn't imagine being part of a team and not talking openly about something so crucial. 'Didn't you share how you were feeling with them at any point…or with anyone else, for that matter?'

Once again he shrugged. 'What was the point? It wasn't going to change our loss. I soon realised that I was wasting energy focusing on my disappointment and that I needed to concentrate on the end goal—to bring a gold medal back to Monrosa. After the first bid we reviewed every aspect of our training plan, from our nutrition to our race schedule. And it worked. We became a much stronger team. From a defeat you can become stronger, if you focus on what you want to achieve.'

He was shifting the conversation away from the fact that he didn't talk to anyone about how crushed he must have felt after the first bid. No doubt deliberately. Could she push him on it? How would he react if she did? Why did this feel like such a tightrope of an interview? What did it say about their relationship that she was so worried about driving him back beyond the wall of silence he so favoured, by asking him to explore in greater depth his thoughts and feelings? This was crazy…she had a job to do. 'Can I take you back to the fact that you didn't talk to anyone about how you were feeling during that time…didn't you find that difficult? Didn't it make it worse not being able to talk about it?'

Ivo frowned at her question and for a moment she thought he was going to gloss over it, but then with a minute shake of his head he answered, 'At the time I was of the mind frame that no amount of talking would make a difference—' he paused and smiled '—but thanks to the last few days with you I'm starting to appreciate that sharing experiences can be beneficial.'

She grinned at that, blushed even. 'It's a careful balance between protecting yourself and honesty, isn't it?' Holding his gaze, the intimacy of their lovemaking so vivid and poignant, she admitted, 'I know you probably won't agree but on balance I think I'd prefer to lead an open life.'

'Actually I do think you're right…it's the braver option, to be open.'

Taken aback by his words, she studied him for a moment and asked, 'Do you really?'

He nodded. 'Yes.'

She had to remember her listeners. Would any of this make any sense to them? She needed to ask him direct and challenging questions that pushed him to be more open, but inside she rebelled at the thought that she might upset the sensitive balance between them. She gritted her teeth, realising that she was scared of giving him a reason to walk away from her. Was what was between them so delicate, so easily broken? 'You were given the nickname the Machine because of your reputation for being impenetrable. Are you saying that you wished you were more open...or that you want to be in the future?'

'I'm private by nature and it has served me in the past...but as my life and career change I'm starting to appreciate the need for openness as well. Whether I can translate that understanding into actual behaviour, time will tell.' He gave her a wry smile. 'As they say, old habits die hard.'

'Who in your life do you want to be more open with?'

Her question earned her another wry smile. 'Thanks to our interviews, I guess I now have the opportunity to be more open with the wider world. I'm talking about aspects of my life that I've never shared before. But it's with those close to me, my family in particular, that I realise that I need a more forthright relationship.'

She nodded encouragingly, wanting him to say more, trying to ignore the thought that she wished he would say that he wanted a closer relationship with her, but hating herself for having such a ridiculous wish when Ivo had never given her any reason to hope for such a thing happening. And mentally she performed an eye roll, frustrated with herself for yet again trying to camouflage her own insecurities by the lure of the distraction and safety of a relationship.

She almost sighed in relief when Ivo spoke again, glad that at least he was moving the interview along and not getting bogged down in rambling inner thoughts as she was. 'Because I attended boarding school as a teenager and then my rowing career dominated my life in the following years, my relationship with my family is somewhat distant, and it's something I know I need to address.'

She was glad. She gave him an encouraging smile, the tension in his expression lightening. She studied her notes, not wanting to think that from tomorrow, other than what she would glean from conversations with Alice and Kara, she would never know how his attempts to connect with his family would fare. She was in regular contact with her previous interviewees but right now she wasn't certain what type of relationship she would manage to foster with Ivo going forward. 'Given the sacrifices a rowing career demands, what was your motivation for wanting to win a gold medal?'

'I'm incredibly proud to be from Monrosa and I wanted to be able to give something back to the people. I wanted to be able to win a medal for the country.'

'Dedicating your life for the best part of a decade to achieving that for your country takes huge self-discipline and sacrifice. Do you ever regret it, or did you even question it when you were in the middle of it all?'

Ivo shook his head. 'No. I'm deeply conscious and appreciative of the privileges afforded me by my position in the Monrosian royal family. I hope that in my athletic career and now in my advisory role in the

Treasury that I can contribute to Monrosa's success and identity.' Pausing, he rubbed his neck. 'I prefer to lead a low-profile life. It's my hope that the public can understand my preference for such a life but know that Monrosa is very important and an integral part of me. Now that I'm living here full-time, I truly appreciate what an incredible country it is. I want to see the country continue to thrive.' He was visibly emotional when he added, 'I'm very proud of all of the changes Edwin is making and want to continue to be part of ensuring the country's continued success.'

For a moment she hesitated in responding, wondering if she was about to destroy just how engaged Ivo was with the interview. And destroy that fragile openness between them. 'The people of Monrosa and external commentators were shocked when your father announced his abdication. Were you? And what do you think his legacy is?'

He frowned at her question, his gaze cooling. She resisted the urge to ask him another question, to smooth away the sudden tension between them, wanting to test how much he was prepared to accept her probing, how much he was prepared to be truly honest with her.

'Yes, I was shocked.' His voice was terse.
'Why?'

Her heart thumped to see his expression tighten. She had lost him. But still she forced herself to hold his gaze, tilting her head upwards, daring him to push her away.

His gaze narrowed but then he answered, 'Being monarch was everything to him. Even more so after the death of my mother. It gave him purpose. I never thought he would be prepared to walk away from that, but he did in order to see Monrosa prosper, believing that the country needed more energy and ideas from a younger monarch. I admire him for taking such a difficult personal decision for the greater good.'

Stopping, he considered her for long moments before adding, 'The following is off the record.'

When she nodded her acceptance, he grimaced and added, 'But that was not the only reason why my father abdicated. He also did so in order to force Edwin to marry and to have children.'

Had she heard right? 'Force him to marry?'

'Edwin and Kara…it was an arranged marriage.'

'No! But they are crazy about one another.' She stopped, realising that she was suddenly close to tears. He had to be making this up. None of this made sense. Kara's marriage couldn't be a sham. If it was…then what hope did anyone else have?

'They were always crazy about one another…but it took my father's interference for them to wake up to that fact.'

'Are you saying that he orchestrated the whole thing?'

'I don't know…perhaps. He definitely wanted heirs to the throne… My father has many faults but he did love my mother greatly. I believe he wanted the same for Edwin.'

'And for you and Luis?'

He gave a brief nod yes. And she swallowed at the thought that Ivo's father wanted him to marry. She pretended to draw a line through some of her questions, trying not to think about sitting and watching Ivo's televised wedding. He might be insistent right now that he didn't want to marry, but, with time and pressure from his father, would he eventually relent?

She needed to ask him another question but, meeting his gaze, she felt her heart lurch, realising that he had just told her something deeply personal and private. Biting her lip, she longed to ask him why he had shared it with her, but, fearing that she would sound needy and that the question would only serve her own vanity and insecurities, she said instead, not stopping to think about the wisdom of doing so, 'You'd be a great dad...if you ever decide to be one.'

He raised a disbelieving eyebrow.

'But you would... I've seen you with Gabriela. You're as soft as putty around her. If I hadn't seen you with my own eyes and got to know you better this weekend I would have said that maybe you would be a distant dad, a little too rigid and strict. But now I know that you would be calm and strong and stable.'

He gave what almost looked like a regretful smile but then shrugged it off, gesturing to her notebook. 'I think we should get back to the main interview.'

She nodded and scanned her list, trying to decide what her next question should be while her mind whirred with a multitude of contemplations.

Did he believe her when she said he'd be a good father? Did he trust and value her opinion enough to listen to what she said? Why was she saying any of this anyway? What was she trying to achieve? What type of mother did he think she would be?

Her brain felt such a mess. This was supposed to be about her having fun, accepting the joy of a short-term affair. She wasn't supposed to be overthinking it all or placing too much importance on what was only a fleeting, joyous outtake on normal life. She needed to get back to the task at hand—now.

'Going back to what you said earlier about public life—do you feel pressure to lead a more public and open life?'

'I appreciate how important the monarchy is in Monrosian life and I understand why the public and media want to see and have access to the royal family. But I'm a private person by nature and prefer to lead a more low-profile life.'

'Have there been times when you have found public life particularly demanding?'

'Obviously the scrutiny and commentary after our first failed international bid was at times difficult.' He considered her for a moment and her heart missed a beat at the emotion that swirled between them in those few seconds. 'But it was in the aftermath of my mother's death that I struggled most with having to maintain a public presence.'

His heart was hammering in his chest. He couldn't believe he was actually admitting all of this. He was supposed to be stoic and never, ever confess to struggling or personal failures. It would be so easy to blame Toni and her questions that went far beyond anything any other journalist had asked of him before. But in truth he wanted to speak, he wanted to be honest about the strains caused by not being able to be true to himself. He wanted others to understand that they were not alone in needing to find self-acceptance. It was as though Toni had unlocked something in him. Was it how natural and good it felt to have someone else in the *finca*, despite all of his initial reservations about it? Or was it how physically depleted he felt after their endless lovemaking? Or how emotionally calm he felt after looking into her eyes time and time again as their bodies joined, her soft smiles of delight, how eagerly she had accepted his kisses and touches, no barriers, no tension existing between them? Just absolute acceptance of the intimate moments they were sharing.

'Do you want to speak about your mum?'

He closed his eyes, decades-old grief catching him by surprise at her softly spoken question. But he wasn't the only one to lose a parent...people were going through it right now and just maybe he could help them understand that there was no right or wrong way to grieve. 'After she died I was incredibly confused and of course extremely sad. At first I was too shocked to talk, and when I was ready to speak those around me were in different places in their own grieving. I think any parents or carers listening should allow their child to grieve at their own pace and in their own way. At the start I needed time alone to process what was happening... but that was not the case for others in my family who needed to be surrounded by people. There's no one way to grieve and I think there needs to be more awareness and understanding of that fact. Always respect where the person is, but also make them aware that you are there when they are ready to talk.'

'Did you talk to anyone when your mum died?'

He gave a regretful shrug. 'For a long time I wasn't ready…and the people closest to me were struggling too.' He stopped, remembering his father's acceptance yesterday when he said he was going to speak about all of this. He could choose to be angry over his father's impatient fury back then, his insistence on following royal protocol and doing what was right publicly as opposed to what was right for his own sons, but to do so would benefit no one. He *had* to make this new-found openness work for everyone's benefit.

'For a long time I believed that shutting down and denying my feelings was the easiest way to cope. But it comes at a price and for me it was a gulf that developed between me and my family. Because I shut down I couldn't engage with them and it was easier to isolate myself from others because then I didn't have to deal with the regrets and guilt that come from distancing yourself.'

'Why guilt?'

Dio! Did she have all day? What son wanted to be a disappointment to his father? What brother wanted to witness his siblings' concern? To know that they pitied him? And then there was all of the guilt of having abandoned his mother, knowing that there was no one at her side when she died. And worst of all the guilt of knowing that if he hadn't begged his mother to go trekking with him that day, if he hadn't raced ahead, then just maybe she could still have been alive. But he wasn't going to load all that on Toni or her listeners. What would be the point? What good could come from laying out all of his failings for others to pick over?

I needed to withdraw within myself to cope with everything that happened but for various reasons it went on too long—my own inclination to be private, the fact that we were sent away to boarding school at a young age. I used to think that the resilience I learnt in how to deal with life on my own was entirely positive, but increasingly I am appreciating the benefit of connecting with others, of being there for them too. It's something I want to rectify with my family. I don't want past tensions to affect the next generation.'

Toni smiled and his heart tightened at the warm empathy shining in her eyes. She lowered her gaze for a moment, before asking softly, 'What are your hopes for the future?'

Up until a few days ago he could have answered that question easily. To grow Pacolore Investments to ensure that he could employ even more a diverse range of people to careers that truly challenged them, and to support local communities within Monrosa in the rejuvenation of forgotten towns and villages. But after this weekend with Toni, realising just how good it was to have company in the *finca*, the question of personal hopes was suddenly on the agenda, but articulating them when he wasn't certain what it was he actually wanted was not something he wanted to think about right now, never mind talk about. 'I have a very fulfilling life at the moment. There isn't much I want to change other than spending more time with my family.'

Toni nodded. But there was a reticence in the way she smiled at him before asking,

'Will you talk to us again in the future? I'm sure the listeners would like to hear how you are doing.'

Why was he grinning at the prospect of another interview with Toni? After all, he hated interviews. But the idea lightened something in him…bringing a feeling of hope, the sense of a future he hadn't imagined for himself. Inhaling, he knew he needed to hold tight to himself all those crazy thoughts and messy emotions Toni was eliciting in him. He folded his arms. 'Does that mean another four-day interview?'

'We can do it whatever way you want—by phone if you'd prefer it that way.' She shrugged as though to say it was of no consequence to her what way they did it. Was that how she really felt? Didn't she want to see him again? Was catching up with him truly just for the podcast?

Shifting closer to the microphone, she spoke directly into it. 'My time with Prince Ivo is drawing to a close here on Monrosa. Thank you for your hospitality…' Her gaze settling on him, she frowned, her smile wavering before she reached and pressed some buttons on the recording equipment. Standing, she quickly started to pack things away. 'I usually do a summary of my time spent with my podcast guest to round off the interview,' glancing outside, she added, 'but, as it's such a nice day, it'd be a shame not to make the most of it. I can record my summary in London next week.'

He could tell that she didn't want to do the summary for reasons other than making the most of the day. He rolled his neck, suddenly tense. What would she say about him? Would she speak negatively about his way of life? Pass judgement on him personally? 'How are you going to summarise your stay here?'

Closing the zip of her laptop bag, she inhaled a long breath. 'I don't know… I need some time to process the whole weekend.' She rolled her eyes. 'I think the lack of sleep is messing with my ability to think straight.' Lowering her eyelids, she shrugged before adding, 'Everything feels very confused right now.'

The low sadness in her voice felt like a stab to his heart. He got her confusion. His own ability to think straight was long gone. And panic, that he might significantly mess up when it came to Toni, had taken its place. Should he let her go, accept this weekend for what it was, or take the risk of inviting someone into his life? He couldn't believe he was even contemplating doing so.

Toni went and stood by the door out to the terrace, her back to him. Arching her spine, she raised her arms up high, her fingertips touching the top of the doorframe, stretching out. She moved with a slow and graceful fluidity. For a long while she stood there, not moving, content to stare out towards the sea. Had San Jorbo's special magic seeped into her bones too? He smiled at how at peace she seemed…could she be happy here? Or would she soon long for the noise and chaos of city life?

Turning, she took a hair tie from her shorts, pulling her hair back into a ponytail, and smiled so tenderly and intimately at him that his heart sang with a happiness so deep he knew that he had to find a way to keep her in his life.

Shading her eyes with her hand, Toni looked in the direction Ivo was pointing towards. 'San Amaro Chapel. Princess Isabella funded its construction in the sixteenth century, ordering that it should be built on the most westerly point of the island. She wanted it to be the symbol of welcome to all returning seafarers.'

The small whitewashed chapel had a golden dome that glowed brightly under the relentless sun, and from their vantage point in the hills to its rear Toni could see a group of people milling around outside, their cars parked along the narrow, single-vehicle road that ran beside it.

They followed the track down to join the road, clusters of red rhododendrons flame-like in amongst the otherwise endless dusty green of the open countryside, no other building to be seen for miles. In the distance, the Mediterranean glistened, the vast sapphire sea competing with the endless azure sky. She loved this island. Especially this remote coastline. It soothed something in her, gave her an inner peace, a grounding that had previously eluded her. She got why Ivo loved the solitude of San Jorbo—being immersed in nature and silence allowed for reflection and growth and it was something she knew she wanted in her life going forward. But would she ever be able to return to Monrosa again? Would it carry too many bittersweet memories?

Ivo led the way, stopping to help her clamber over a heavy rockfall, asking gently, 'Are you okay? Do you need some water, a break?'

She nodded no, then gave him a grateful smile, pretending, pretending, pretending that all was well.

When he turned away she slowly exhaled, watching his long, agile strides.

Don't think. Don't start hoping and dreaming. Don't confuse the easy connection of a casual hook-up with anything more than that. You spent too many years willing for things to be different with Dan, clinging to your relationship, to go back now into a situation full of uncertainty and doubt and misguided hope.

As they approached the church, the group outside turned in their direction, their expressions moving from surprise to delight on spotting Ivo. The men were dressed in tuxedos, the women in cocktail dresses, rows of potted lemon trees lining the red carpet. A wedding. One of the younger men approached them, his smile infectious. He had to be the groom.

With much excitement he introduced Ivo to his family and then insisted that they accompany him into the chapel, Ivo translating for her that the groom wanted to show them the flowers he had secretly organised for his bride. Toni gasped at the delicate beauty of the pink and cream tea roses that filled every available space of the tiny chapel, their scent exquisite.

And then the rest of the group bustled in, quickly taking their places. The bride had arrived.

Outside, Ivo spoke to the bride and her family and friends, the bride blushing with pleasure at Ivo's good wishes. And Toni's heart cracked open at how deliberately Ivo took his time, speaking not only with the bride but also her parents, who looked ecstatic to have the good fortune to have a member of the beloved royal family give them his good wishes.

Ivo may not enjoy public life in its more intrusive forms, but on a one-to-one level he showed incredible humility and warmth.

And as they stood and watched the bride

enter the chapel, a solo guitarist inside heralding her arrival, Toni turned and studied Ivo, and, though she wanted nothing more than to stay one more night with him, she realised it was time that she leave, before she lost her heart and all reason to him.

From the chapel they followed the road down to the coast and then walked along the track that skirted along the coastline and would eventually lead them back to San Jorbo.

'Are you okay? You seem distracted.'

He shrugged at Toni's question, trying not to give way to the panic growing inside of him. 'I'm thinking about the week ahead—the markets were jittery last week because of a disruption in oil production.'

He caught Toni's frown. She didn't believe him. *Dio!* How could he tell her the truth? How could he tell her that earlier he had actually been considering broaching the idea that they meet up again, possibly even date? What they had was good. But now he knew just how nonsensical that idea was. He and Toni had no future together. She deserved something better than a man who could never fully engage in a relationship. He would never be a man so certain, so safe and assured in a relationship that he would beam with happiness on his wedding day. Relationships, permanency, the need to be honest and frank were beyond him. He lived in his own thoughts, he hated being emotionally vulnerable. He wasn't capable of loving a woman the way a man should.

At a fork in the path, they came to a stop and studied the beach below them in silence. He had said that they would have a picnic there and he wanted to go and lie down with her, listen to her chatter and laughter, and lose himself in their kisses and touches. But instead he glanced at his watch. 'This has taken us longer than I thought. I need to get back to the *finca*. The financial markets abroad are open today.'

He hated the disappointment that clouded her eyes. But then with a firm nod of her head she stepped away. 'Of course...actually that suits me, as I've decided that, now that our interview is finished, I'll change my flight home to London to today. It makes sense as you're busy.'

* * *

Toni forced herself to smile through his shocked expression. Pretending, pretending, pretending that going home was exactly what she wanted to do instead of longing for him to ask her to stay. She wanted to stay and watch him shower in the morning, load his toast with honey the way he liked it, hear his serious voice on the phone when he talked business, his sharp intelligence and decisiveness a crazy turn-on. She wanted to spend more evenings playing with Paco and Lore with him, hearing his laughter when one of the dogs easily beat her in the game of catch the four of them played together. She wanted to make love with him time and time again. It was too soon to say goodbye to the ecstasy, the freedom, the rightness they found together. Another few days. That was all she wanted.

'If that's what you want.'

Her heart sank. His tone was distant and cool.

She faked another smile. 'I think it's for the best.'

She backed away and turned in the direction they had been walking. It felt as though a tidal wave of disappointment was pushing against her back, driving her forward.

What did you expect? It was your suggestion that you leave. Don't you want to be in control? You said you wanted to wear relationships lightly, not get emotionally involved.

But I thought we had something special... I thought he felt it too. More than just chemistry...love. I'm in love with him.

There. She had thought it. She was in love with him. How unbelievably stupid.

Oh, come on, Toni. Think about it. Are you really in love with him? How about testing that idea? What would you do if he called to you right now and asked you to stay? You would be thrilled, of course... for about five minutes. And then you'd panic. Panic because you wouldn't know if you could really believe him. Because you couldn't handle being in a relationship again with all the potential hurt and pain that goes with that. Because you know you'd always be waiting for the day he would walk away. Just like Dan. Just like your dad. You love him...but you'd always be scared of what he could do, scared of the pain he could inflict on you. You'd never feel safe with him. Would you really want that life?

On the phone to his Global Emerging Markets team, Ivo tried to concentrate but his head was a jumble of thoughts. She was leaving. He should be glad. It was all too intense and out of control. It had to end, and probably the sooner the better, before he indulged any further in fantasies of waking next to her in the mornings, arriving home to her smiles and chatter, the long hours of lovemaking where the connection between them bound his heart with a sense of peace and belonging and joy.

Her eagerness to leave cut him to the quick. Yes, he knew that he couldn't offer her the love she needed, the openness and absolute conviction that any relationship needed...but her ability to walk away so easily was causing the walls of silence around him to firmly shift back into place.

Twisting in his chair, he saw Toni standing at his office door. Her hair was damp and she had changed into the yellow dress she had worn on her first day in Monrosa.

How long had she been standing there? Her eyes held his for the briefest of moments and he swallowed at the confusion in their depths.

But then she gave him a cheerful smile and mouthed if she could speak to him for a few seconds?

Telling his team that he would call them back, he waited for her to speak.

She took a step into the office but then stepped away again, as though she didn't want to be in the same room as him, despite her persistent smile. 'You'll be glad to hear that I've managed to change my flight. I'm packed and ready to go.'

He stood. 'You're leaving now?' He had thought she would leave tonight. Not immediately. Just how keen was she to escape?

'Yeah, my taxi should be here any minute now.' She smiled again, upbeat and positive, as though all of this was a brilliant idea. 'You'll be glad to have me out of your hair, no doubt.' Nodding towards his laptop, she added, 'At least now you'll have some peace to concentrate on work.'

He should be relieved. At least now he wouldn't have to spend the rest of the day resisting the temptation of asking her to stay, of saying that they would figure something out. But to what end? He stared at her, his brain a jumble of messy thoughts, panic closing down any logical thinking.

'I had hoped we could talk later...'

She folded her arms. 'About what?'

He moved towards her, needing somehow to make this all okay. 'The past few days have been special...thank you. I hope you think so too.'

She shrugged, backing away and then, glancing out of the window behind her, she said with obvious relief, 'My taxi is here.'

He watched her dart down the corridor, bewildered by the suddenness of all this. He gathered himself enough to follow her, taking hold of the suitcase on the floor. She opened the front door without looking at him and instinctively he reached out, stopping her from opening it in full. Outside he could hear the low rumble of a car engine.

'Stay. Let's talk.'

She shook her head. 'Thanks but I really want to get back to London.' Meeting his gaze, she winced ever so slightly before she pulled at the door, edging it a little more open, her demeanour and tone still forcibly bright and cheerful. 'Thanks for a lovely weekend.' She lifted the bag that contained all of the recording equipment. 'I'll edit your interview and send you a copy some time this week or next.' Then, holding her hand out, she gave him yet another bright smile. 'Thank you for participating in the interview.' As she paused, heat crept into her cheeks but a defiant glint entered her eyes. 'And thanks for everything else...it was fun.'

'You don't need to leave now.'

Her smile faded. 'Yes, I do.'

'Why?'

She studied him, her expression crumbling. 'Please, Ivo... I'm trying to make this as easy as possible for us both.'

He stepped away, nodding. She was right. It wasn't her problem that he felt totally ill-equipped to deal with the fall-out of growing so extraordinarily close to another human being. For so many years he had deliberately isolated himself and in a matter of days Toni had destroyed the comfort and security that had come with that detachment, leaving him feeling more vulnerable now than he had ever felt in his entire life.

Outside, she got into the waiting taxi.

Stupidly he waved, as though that was appropriate or somehow could convey how he wanted to reach out to her, to say he was sorry, and she responded with a saddened shrug that perfectly summed up her disappointment in him.

Paco and Lore chased after the taxi as it twisted away into the olive groves. Just as he should have done, if he weren't so inhibited by the inability to love without reservation.

CHAPTER NINE

TONI STUMBLED INTO the kitchen and sighed at the breakfast detritus her flatmates had left behind them before they had rushed out to work.

Wincing, she checked the time on her phone charging on the kitchen counter. It was past ten o'clock. She hadn't intended on staying out so late last night, just as she hadn't intended on staying out late every night of the past week, but she had always managed to find some excuse to avoid the awfulness of lying in bed unable to sleep, thinking about Ivo.

Walking into the living room, she eyed the recording equipment sitting on her desk. Two weeks had passed since she'd recorded Ivo's interview. She was scheduled to broadcast it in two days' time but had yet to edit it. She had found every excuse in the book to avoid listening to it—editing prior interviews, creating a new marketing strategy for the podcast with the PR department at Young Adults Together, cleaning the flat, dragging her flatmates out to parties and gallery openings and drinks in the pub.

But now she had no choice but to edit it today. She had to send it to the palace and Ivo later today to get their approval, and tomorrow she was flying to Amsterdam for another interview. She should be excited. She hadn't visited Amsterdam in years. But, as with everything else in her life right now, no matter how much she tried to deny it, the joy had gone out of everything she did. She felt flattened. Why had she gone and fallen in love with him? Why hadn't she been able to not get entangled with him emotionally? Had she allowed the seclusion, the intimacy of his *finca*, to create a make-believe world that never had a chance of surviving? Had she totally imagined the connection between them? Had it simply been a case of a whole lot of chemistry and very little else for him?

She sighed, remembering the phone calls from Kara and Alice after she had returned to London. Both had wanted to know in great detail how the interview had gone and if she had anything to do with the fact that Ivo was rarely returning to San Jorbo and instead was staying in the palace most evenings. Neither had been subtle in their questioning, Kara eventually admitting that she had hoped that they might get together. Toni had laughed off the suggestion, pointing out the fact that they had so little in common. But Kara had argued that they would balance each other out perfectly. Toni had ended their call at that point, unable to handle Kara's disappointment that her matchmaking had come to nothing. By rights she should be angry with Kara, but who could blame her friend for hoping that those in her life had the same happiness and contentment that her marriage brought her?

Wiping down the kitchen table and counters while she waited for the kettle to boil, Toni knew she couldn't put off editing Ivo's interview any longer.

Coffee cup in hand, she went and sat at her desk. Pulling on her headphones, she selected the first recording in his office, grimacing at the overexcited nervousness in her voice, her heart turning over at his concise replies.

He had stood on his doorstep and waved her goodbye. While she had sat in the taxi, her heart breaking, he had waved her off the way you would a favourite aunt. That had summed up just how easy he had found it when she had left. And he had been right... after all, he had stuck to their deal that there would be no entanglements, just fun. She only had herself to blame. At least she had had the sense to get out of there early. When they had returned to San Jorbo after their trek to San Amaro he had instantly disappeared into his office and she had crazily toyed with the idea of going in and telling him what he meant to her. To what purpose she had no real idea. It was just her usual need to overshare, to wear her heart on her sleeve rearing its idiotic head. Thankfully she had resisted the temptation to emotionally unburden herself to him, realising she would only hurt and humiliate herself in the process. And had poured her nervous energy into changing her flight and packing instead. Needing to take control of the whole situation. Needing to be the one who

walked away, rather than being so danger-
ously close to jumping into yet another relationship which had gaping holes in its very
foundations.

Now she closed her eyes at his mention
of ice-cream and olive oil in the interview,
remembering how he had teased her on the
beach. He had never shown her what other
uses olive oil could be put to. She pushed
away the mental image of him rubbing the
golden liquid into her skin…and what would
follow as a result.

Her coffee grew cold as she listened to his
voice, every sense awake to him, stopping to
edit out silences and parts of the interview
that didn't flow with the overall structure.

*'I needed time alone to process what was
happening.'*

She pressed 'pause' at the point in the interview when he had talked about the aftermath of his mum's death, closing her eyes,
trying to think.

A glimmer of hope had her heart doing a
cartwheel. Did he just need time? Maybe he
would realise that what they had was special. Ugh! Why was she even thinking this
way? Why was she so desperate for him to

love her? She had stayed with Dan because it had felt safer to do so. Was that why she'd fallen so hard and fast for Ivo, because she'd simply wanted the security of a relationship? Did she truly love Ivo…or was it the thought of a relationship that she loved even more? But relationships terrified her, so why would she even subconsciously want to be in one? Her head was such a mess. How could she long for something that also terrified her?

She pulled out her headphones and went and stood at the bay window overlooking the street below her. Cars were parked along either side of the tree-lined pavement but there wasn't a soul in sight.

She hated being alone because it reminded her of all the times that her dad had disappeared from her life. The confusion, the wondering of what she had done wrong. She had never felt safe because of it. But in bed with Ivo, when they made love, for the first time ever she *had* felt safe. In their walks, their time on the beach, she had felt safe in his silence, in how he had made no demands of her but simply looked at her as though she was the most wonderful person he had ever encountered. She hadn't imagined that…she was certain of it. She might fool herself over many other things in her life, but Ivo's look of care and fondness wasn't one of them.

But she couldn't force him to love her, to want a life he had never envisioned for himself. And she had to stop being so afraid of being alone. She needed to learn to feel safe in her own life.

Ivo stood on the *finca*'s terrace as Paco and Lore raced down the path to the beach. Palace life didn't suit them. Their movements were too restricted and there were too many people shooing them out of the way. At least they were happy to be back in San Jorbo. His gaze trailed over the beach below, the memories of making love to Toni down there grabbing his heart, and the real reason why he had avoided returning to San Jorbo for the past two weeks. Sure, he had stayed in the palace in order to spend time with his family, but avoiding memories of Toni had been the main reason why time and time again he had delayed his return home. Most evenings he had managed to return to the palace in time to say goodnight to Gabriela, sharing a beer with Edwin afterwards, chatting about the most recent economic news, acting as a sounding board for Edwin's concerns over the Monrosian economy. And after that he would visit Luis and Alice in their villa in the grounds of the palace, more often than not staying for dinner, getting much needed light relief in the constant teasing banter they drew him into, Luis, ever the competitor, challenging him to compete against him in triathlons, insisting he was the fitter of them both. And afterwards he would sometimes drop in to see his father. They had been uncomfortable visits, awkward after so many years of distance. But he was tired of pretending he didn't need a relationship with his father. Because he did. He needed his guidance...his love. He needed to belong to his family.

The sun was fading. He should go for a swim before night fell. But instead he closed his eyes, listened to the cicadas, waiting for the wash of peace that usually came when he returned to San Jorbo after the chaos of a working day.

But the image of Toni, sitting next to him in the studio that first night she arrived, enthusiastically embracing his art, haunted him. He had shown her who he was. Private. Introverted. Damaged. Not an easy person to live with. And she had accepted him. On their last day together, when she had interviewed him for the podcast he had seen with his own eyes how carefully she'd tried to balance his need for privacy with her own need for an in-depth interview. Why, then, had he shut down the moment she announced that she was leaving? Did asking her to stay terrify him that much? Was he so conditioned to a single life that it was intractable now? But he had to face facts—he could never give her his absolute conviction in the truth and rightness of their relationship. Could you really commit to a relationship if you didn't believe in your own capacity to honour the openness and honesty that were fundamental to its survival?

But hadn't her hope and belief in him been what he had been searching for all his life? Someone who believed in him? Someone who had the same hopes and dreams for a shared future?

He threw his head back and studied the darkening sky, Venus shining as brilliantly and defiantly as ever.

He didn't want to be alone. His mother had died so young…she had had so many years of happiness robbed from her. Years of seeing her sons grow up. Years of loving the husband who idolised her. She had been robbed of seeing the birth of her first grandchild.

He may not have been able to save her the day of her fall, but he could honour her memory a whole lot better than he was doing right now.

He needed to be true to himself. He needed to admit that he wanted love…and to be loved. He closed his eyes. What if she didn't want his love? And didn't love him? When they had made love, when she would touch him whenever she passed him, when he caught her staring at him, when she gave him her absolute attention as though validating everything that was him, all those things had felt like real and meaningful love. He wasn't used to listening to his instincts, preferring logic instead. But deep inside of him, if he discarded his entrenched fears for a moment, he believed that Toni did love him.

He had to tell her what was truly inside him. Every fear and failure, every hope and dream for their future. He needed to speak. But above all else he needed to be fair. And his silence and withdrawal weren't fair on her.

He worked his jaw in frustration. He knew how hurt she was over her relationship with Dan. The damage her father had inflicted on her. He knew how sensitive she was, her need for assurance. To feel safe.

And he had failed to meet every single need she had from a relationship in his silence. He hadn't given her the lifelines, the essential components, which any relationship needed but were even more vital to Toni—true intimacy, security, trust and honesty. He wanted to make amends for how he had messed up...but what if he couldn't? What if she didn't want him to? Worst of all, what if he was the totally wrong person for her? What if she needed a more sensitive, more giving, less complicated person? What if he couldn't make her happy?

With her flight not for another few hours, Toni had planned on visiting the Rijksmuseum, but the long line of queuing tourists had had her turn away.

Her interview with renowned chef Evi Kaag had been stimulating and thought-provoking. Evi's passionate creativeness in the kitchen was matched by her dedication to mentoring her staff to exacting standards whilst also allowing them the space to experiment and fulfil their own creative needs. A mum of three, Evi, together with her husband Christian, had created a home full of love and laughter. But Evi had spoken candidly about how she struggled to balance all of the demands in her life, her regrets over her first marriage failing and her ongoing worry of caring for her elderly parents.

It had been an open and frank interview and had driven home just how tense and awkward her interviews with Ivo had been. Okay, so towards the end he had opened up, but had she really got to know him? Her time with Evi had increased an underlying nagging doubt that she still truly didn't know the man nicknamed the Machine.

And yet, despite all of that, she missed him. She missed his calmness, his warm looks that made every inch of her skin fizzle and her heart dance with joy, his kindness and humanity. She missed his quiet solidness, how he tried to be true to himself, how little ego he had.

Walking over a pedestrian bridge, bicycles whizzing by, she spotted a free bench along the canalside and dragged her suitcase over to it. Sitting down, she heard her phone ping in her handbag. It was yet another message from Kara, wondering if she was still with Evi. She typed no, explaining that earlier Evi and her family had left for their holiday home on the island of Ameland and that she was currently enjoying the views alongside the Herengracht canal, desperate to appear upbeat even if inside she felt numb.

As she popped her phone back into her handbag her attention was drawn to a young couple sitting on a bench on the opposite side of the canal. She could tell by their gentle teasing and tentative touching that their relationship was new. And the sensation that something extremely precious had escaped her came back with a vengeance. Along with the question that if life had been different for them both, could their relationship have been as easy and natural as it was for the couple across the way? Would she and Ivo have glided into a relationship without any reservations? How wonderful it must be to be able to love without hesitation, to be able to accept love with an open heart.

'I was looking for you.'

She leapt off the bench. And stared at Ivo. Her heart lurching in disbelief. 'Did you have to creep up on me like that?'

Her shock evaporated in the face of his sombre expression. She swallowed hard. The dappled shade of a nearby tree cast shadows over the hard lines of his face. Her heart stumbled and tripped. He looked so foreboding, so tense, so cut off from her.

He gestured to the bench. 'Let's sit down.'

She nodded but dread started to settle in her stomach. Why was he being so formal?

Sitting, she inched away from him when he sat close to her, the distance suddenly of vital importance. The need to protect herself from whatever was to come panicking her.

'Is this about the podcast? Your office said you were happy for it to be broadcast. Was your father unhappy with it? I know it was revealing, but the feedback has been incredible. Ask Kara.'

'I'm not here about the interview… I'm here to apologise.'

Toni's eyes widened. 'For what? And how did you find me in the first place?'

'Kara.'

'So that's what all of her messages were about.' But then, her eyes widening even more, she asked, clearly horrified, 'How did you explain wanting to know where I was? That's all I need right now, Kara suspecting something.'

'I told my family about us.'

'Why on earth did you do that? Ivo...seriously! That's going to complicate my life even further. I told Kara and Alice that nothing happened between us. I'm now going to have them on my case. Just great.'

She flicked her gaze away from him, her mouth pursed.

Great start, Ivo.

He dipped his head, the words he needed to say fading, the instinct to lapse into silence when he felt uncertain flooding back with a vengeance. He gripped his fists tight, fighting the fear that he wasn't deserving of her love. That he could never be open enough to match her need for honest transparency.

Searching for the right words, he looked at

her, the hunger of his need to simply watch her stunning him by its ferocity. He had missed her even more than he had admitted to himself. His throat tightened, the true loneliness of her absence intensifying now that he had found her.

The light breeze danced in her hair, sending golden brown strands over her heated cheeks. He had never met someone so beautiful. He prized every tiny detail of her, the ordinary in her a constant source of marvel and worship. The bow in her upper lip. The tight whorl of her ears. The random smattering of dark freckles along her arms. Just how incredible she looked in the simple white T-shirt and jeans she was wearing today.

She turned and gave an exasperated sigh. 'Ivo, are you going to say something or are you just going to sit there and stare at me? For crying out loud, why did you tell your family about me? What was the point?'

'You were the one who said we should be honest.'

'Not about us sleeping together!'

'Well, I obviously didn't tell them that, but I did tell them that we had grown close but that I had messed up…and I wanted to make amends.'

On a deep sigh, she shook her head. 'You didn't mess up, Ivo. It was never going to work between us. We've both got way too much baggage. Let's face facts. We're not good for one another.'

Did she really mean that? What if she was right? But all of those tender moments when they had made love, the laughter they had shared, the quiet understanding that had marked so many moments of their time together…they all had to count for something, didn't they?

'Maybe I'm not right for you, and I guess only you can decide that. It's something I've been worried about too. But I did mess up. I should have asked you to stay in Monrosa. I should have told you what you meant to me but I didn't because I had convinced myself that I was incapable of truly loving another person.'

Her gaze narrowed. 'Why did you believe that?'

'Our time in Monrosa together was incredible, different from anything I had ever experienced before. I loved being with you and I had been planning on suggesting we see each other again. But when we came across the wedding in San Amaro Chapel, the groom was so confident and certain about marrying, it drove home just how inept I was in loving you the way you deserved. Falling in love, truly falling in love, means being open and honest, being capable of showing the other person how much you love them. And we both know just how terrible I am in showing my emotions. To fall in love you should have the capability to love generously, to make the other person feel content and secure. But I was scared that I was too inarticulate, too closed to do any of that. And when you said that you were leaving early I panicked. I messed up, and since you left I've been miserable. I miss you. For so long I thought that I was content alone and that I accepted who I was. But in truth I was lying to myself about just how lonely and isolated I was. I was too scared to reach out to others. I'm tired of living that life, of pretending that I'm okay on my own. I want us to be together. I want us to have a future.'

She shook her head, her expression one of sad resignation. 'On what basis? What did we really have but lots of attraction? Chemistry is no foundation for a relationship.'

'But doesn't that chemistry tell you a lot?'

'No.'

He winced at the defiant certainty of her answer. He fought the instinctive compulsion to withdraw, to close himself off from potential pain and humiliation, and instead said, 'That chemistry confirms that we're right for one another. Our bodies know it… it's just our minds that need to catch up.'

'And what about our hearts?'

He swallowed, the effort to tell the truth inside of him not getting any easier. 'I lost my heart to you at Luis's wedding. As crazy as this may seem, I fell in love with you that day and each hour that I spend with you I fall deeper and deeper in love.'

Her eyebrows shot up. She stared at him for what felt like an eternity. 'You love me? You fell for me at the wedding…but you spent most of the day dodging out of my way whenever I came close to you.'

'I didn't know how to be around you.' He swallowed again, his throat tight, as though his body was mirroring just how painful he found it to reveal the deepest, most personal sides of himself. 'When my mother died I learnt that the easiest way to survive was to ignore my feelings. For years I have used my indifference, my detachment as a shield to not being hurt. And when we met, your openness, how easily you cried and expressed yourself, totally threw me. I didn't know how to react but deep down I admired you for being so open.'

'You admired the fact that I was a red-eyed, bubbling mess?'

'That's not how I remember you—you were outgoing, enthusiastic, you were alive with energy...and you were very, very beautiful.'

Shifting her gaze across the canal towards the young couple entwined in one another, she said in a voice full of sadness and regret, 'But doesn't it worry you that none of this is easy? We both have so many well-founded reasons not to be in a relationship, can we really overcome them?' Looking at him, her brown eyes forlorn, she murmured, 'I'm terrified that I want to be in a relationship for all of the wrong reasons.'

He heard the fear in her voice. A fear he understood, given her background. He needed to turn this around, help her see the reasons why they should fight for what they had. 'Forget all of the wrong reasons for a moment and tell me what the right reasons to be in a relationship are?'

Her head reeling, Toni stared towards the couple across the water. They were sharing one set of earphones, both heads moving in time to music only they could hear. 'The right reasons? I guess the closeness, the intimacy, knowing that there's someone in your corner. An ally and friend you can trust implicitly—' she paused, realisation hitting her '—and by that I mean not only that I can trust *in* them but also that I allow myself to trust them. After my dad and Dan, I'm not sure that I can fully trust someone again and I know that's not fair.'

Ivo shifted towards her, his eyes holding her captive, his voice a soft whisper. 'I want you to be able to trust me.'

She hesitated for a moment but all of the reasons why she hadn't wanted to fall in love again assailed her and she heard herself say, 'I want to trust you but I'm scared of believing you when you say you love me because one day you might decide to leave me and I couldn't abide the hurt and pain of losing you.'

Moving along the bench, Ivo positioned himself at an angle so that his knee was touching hers, his silver gaze holding hers for what felt like an eternity. 'I will never leave you.' His mouth quirked. 'Do you honestly think that I'd leave you after all this? It has almost broken me to admit everything I have... I may be inarticulate about my feelings and closed to my emotions—I've had to fight internal demons, slay decades-old ways of being, to get to this point—but integrity is everything to me and I will never hurt you again. I want your honesty and openness. I want your laughter, your chatter. I'll even put up with your clutter and untidiness.'

Inhaling deeply, she studied him. She knew just how huge it was for him to tell her all of this. To tell her that he loved her. It would be so easy to accept everything he was saying and fall into a fantasy world, but, rightly or wrongly, she needed more from him. 'Sometimes I feel that I don't truly know you, as though you are holding something back from me. Tell me the deepest parts of you. What's your greatest regret?' The need to test him, to see if he would be brutally honest, drove her on to ask, 'Tell me what you want from our relationship and what you are willing to sacrifice for it? What if I want to continue living in London for instance?'

He held up his hand as though to stop her flow of questions. 'I'll answer every question you have...but you need to slow down. Ask me them individually. I want to make sure that I answer every question in detail.'

'Tell me about the deepest regret?'

'Letting you go...but there are many others.' She could see that it was an effort for him to continue as he ran his hand against his neck. Seconds passed and her heart sank. He was avoiding looking at her. Was he already clamming up?

On a heavy exhale his eyes met hers and she flinched at the strain in his expression. 'I regret insisting that my mother take me trekking on the day she died. She had told us that she had a headache. Even knowing that, when we did go I didn't stay with her but rushed ahead. And then when I found her on the ground I ran away, to get help but also because I was so scared. I shouldn't have left her alone to die. And on top of all of that, what I regret most is that she was stolen from my father's and brothers' lives and the guilt of that eats me up. I could see their pain after she died and I couldn't face it, so it was easier to stay in my room and detach myself from them.'

It would be so easy to give a glib response, to try to convince him that he was wrong to feel any responsibility or guilt. And that it was understandable that he struggled with witnessing his family's grief. But to do so would be to disregard and diminish what were clearly very painful feelings for him. 'It's no wonder that you withdrew. What you went through was horrible. I so dearly wish life had been different for you and I'm sorry that you had to carry that responsibility on your own all these years.' Her throat felt too tight to continue as she thought of all the years Ivo had kept his guilt to himself, his natural need for privacy becoming extreme in his grief, and her heart tumbled as she realised what it must have taken him to admit all of this to her. 'Thanks for telling me.'

He nodded and then looked away. Before she would have thought that that act of looking away was him somehow distancing himself from her, but now she recognised that it was a combination of his reserved nature but also his pride and composure. Moving her hand to rest on his, she quietly said, 'Sometimes I've mistaken your quietness for a personal rejection.'

He turned and regarded her. 'It's not intentional…please tell me when you feel that way.'

'Sometimes I don't even understand why I even think you are pushing me away, given just how kind you were to me when we first met.' Closing her eyes, she grimaced and then, looking back at him, she gave a long exhale. 'I should explain why I was so emotional at Alice's wedding. When we danced, the way you held me, the understanding in your voice when we spoke, broke me. I realised just how desperately I wanted to be looked at with that kindness and care. I wanted to truly matter to someone. I wanted to be the centre of someone's life.'

He shifted on the seat towards her and her heart swelled at the tenderness in his eyes.

'You matter to me…and you are already the centre of my life. I love you.'

She blinked back tears, the sincerity in his eyes, the passion in his voice freeing her of all the doubts and misgivings she had been harbouring over entering a relationship again. 'I used to think that love is unreliable, but it's only people that are unreliable, not love. And in our time together you have always been consistent and true, you've always shown me huge respect and integrity. You believed in me. I didn't want to trust you, I was so scared of being hurt again, but not once have you done anything to cause me to doubt your loyalty. Instead you've helped me to learn to appreciate my strengths, and what better way can I prove to myself that I believe in myself than by trusting my judgement and allowing myself to completely trust you?' She paused and with a certainty that brought fresh tears to her eyes she said, 'I love you, Ivo, and want to be with you.'

A look of relief and then joy passed over his features. With a grin he said, 'I can't tell you how good that sounds. Say it again.'

She laughed. 'I love you.'

'And again.'

'I love you.'

He gathered her to him, his kiss quick, reflecting his delight. He was still grinning when he pulled away.

Thinking about how far they had come in truly knowing each other, she said, 'We still have so much to learn and understand about each other...doesn't that worry you?'

He looked out to a passing boat on the canal as he considered her question. 'In truth, I'm only learning about myself now because of you.' Then with a determined expression he added, 'But we *will* be okay. This openness and honesty we have with each other will see us through.'

He was right. This candidness and truth would be the bedrock of their relationship. But even knowing that didn't stop the fluttering of dread that came with her next question. 'What future do you want for us?'

His expression grew tense. For a moment she panicked, thinking he was perhaps about to tell her something she didn't want to hear, but then she realised it was because he was nervous. 'I'd like you to come and live with me in San Jorbo. The land there feels as though it's part of me. I hope that in time you might grow to love it as much as I do. But if you want to live in the palace or stay in London we can make that work too. We would need to travel to Monrosa for my royal duties.'

'I've grown to love Monrosa, and being close to Kara and Alice would be wonderful. I've missed San Jorbo too, but I will need a studio and easy access to the airport for when I travel for my podcast interviews.'

He nodded. 'We can set up a studio in San Jorbo, and when you need to fly any-where we can base ourselves at the palace so that you'll be closer to the airport. And Kara has her offices there too, so you'll be able to work even closer with her.'

'A studio in San Jorbo sounds perfect,' she admitted with a wide smile, 'but be warned I'll drag you to parties every now and again.'

The laughter lines at the corners of his eyes crinkled. 'With you at my side I might even tolerate them, but be warned, I will drag you home from them early...' Heat formed in his eyes and, leaning into her ear, he whispered, 'You're irresistible when you wear lipstick and high heels.'

A thrill torpedoed through her body and another had her physically tremble when his mouth playfully nuzzled against her throat. Her head swimming, she edged closer to him, sighing when his mouth found hers, his gentle kiss electrifying. Pulling back, he held her eyes for long, tender moments before he softly whispered, 'I hope in time that we'll want to leave parties early to get home to our children.'

She gave a cry of surprise that was half shock and half absolute joy. For a moment she wanted to tell him that he was jumping ahead, not wanting to dare to dream of such a future with him, but then she stopped herself, needing to voice the truth of her hopes. 'I can't think of anything more wonderful.'

Looking across the canal again towards the young couple, who were busy taking selfies, Ivo's arm around her shoulders anchoring her to him, she asked, 'Doesn't it scare you that this could so easily not have happened?'

Placing a hand beneath her chin, turning her gaze towards him, he nodded. 'Yes...' his thumb gently moved along her jawline '...and that's why I will never take you or our love for granted.'

* * *

Later that night the silver moon guided them through the olive groves and on through the mountain forest, Paco and Lore leading the way, excited to have another companion on their nightly walk.

Wrapped up in one of his fleece jackets against the chill in the mountain air, her hand in his as they walked side by side, Toni muttered, 'I didn't realise that you walked so far every night… I had thought it would be nothing but a quick leg-stretch.'

He knew that he was probably rushing things, but it felt so right and good and amazing to have her back in his life that he couldn't hold back on sharing the future he wanted them to have. 'There's something I want to show you.'

'Please don't tell me that it's a Monrosian Hairy-Back Spider.'

He laughed at her pretend horror, his heart squeezing at the sheer joy of having her here. And when they reached their destination, a clearing on the edge of the mountain, he pointed across the bay to San Amaro Chapel. All the way here he had waited for his nerves to kick in, for all the old worries about sharing his life with anyone to take over again. But they didn't come. The rightness and the power of their love, the truth and honest connection between them had banished all those fears. 'I'd like us to marry in San Amaro…if you are happy with a small wedding, of course.'

Open-mouthed, Toni stared at him, then towards the chapel, before staring at him again. 'Marry…in San Amaro?'

'I'd like the wedding to be private…and intimate. We can marry in the cathedral if you prefer, but I want to be able to focus just on you on our wedding day, and that's difficult when you have hundreds of guests.'

'You want to marry me? Is this a proposal?'

He laughed at her astonishment. But then, sobering, he realised that perhaps this wasn't the most romantic of ways to propose. He started to backtrack. 'I can do it properly… take you somewhere more romantic, Paris or Venice. And, of course, there's the engagement ring…'

Stepping forward, she placed her hands on his arms, laughter in her eyes. 'I didn't mean it that way. I can't think of a more special place than here, where we will spend our life together. I'm just taken aback that you are proposing now…it's all so sudden.'

Disappointment kicked him in the stomach. 'We can talk about it some other time if you prefer.'

She shook her head firmly, a smile lifting her lips. 'No, no, I don't mean sudden in a bad way, just in an *I didn't expect this from you* sort of way. I'm supposed to be the emotional and impetuous one in this relationship.' Her smile widening even more, those brown eyes of hers gleaming with love and dreams, she said, 'San Amaro would be perfect.'

EPILOGUE

WHEN DESIGNING HER wedding gown, Toni
had asked for pockets in the vintage silk and
lace gown, so that she could carry a handkerchief. She had been convinced that she
would cry endlessly.

Admittedly, she had shed a tear when Alice
and Kara had joined her this morning, both
of them looking radiant in their blush-pink
bridesmaid gowns, Alice in particular, her
eight-month pregnancy bump swathed beneath the soft silk folds of her gown. And
a lump had formed in her throat when she
had stood at the end of the short aisle of San
Amaro and taken her mother's arm, seeing
the natural beauty of the chapel enhanced
with the white rose and olive branch floral
displays.

The wide smiles of their small group of
wedding guests—her friends from Lon-

don, Ivo's rowing team and university friends he was in regular contact with— had also threatened her composure. But now, taking the light cotton and lace handkerchief from her pocket wasn't for her tears but for Ivo's.

Reluctantly taking the handkerchief from her, Ivo quickly wiped his eyes, ignoring the amused looks of his brothers and best men, Edwin and Luis, both dressed in tuxedos, as were the rest of their male guests. In her father's arms, Gabriela, wearing the same simple floral crown of white roses as Toni's in her dark hair, gave a chortle, and the rest of the guests chuckled. Ivo shook his head, his watery eyes filled with amusement, and then he softly whispered, 'I love you.'

From the altar the priest cleared his throat. 'Shall we start again?'

They both nodded, but in truth she was in no rush. She wanted to enjoy every second of this ceremony, savour every minute of this extraordinary day.

Looking down at the vows he had written himself, Ivo cleared his throat and this time managed to say the words without his voice cracking. 'You are the centre of my world. You bring me joy, acceptance and contentment. Every day throughout our marriage I promise to hear and react to your feelings and thoughts. I vow to love, respect, and cherish you. I pledge myself only to you, as long as we both shall live.'

Her heart filled with love, Toni repeated her own vows, her voice steady, not even a single tear in her eye, her safety and security in their relationship, Ivo time and time again proving over the past year of their life together in San Jorbo that she was the centre of his world, his constant gentle kindness, their intimate lovemaking, freeing her of any doubts as to his love.

And after her vows, Ivo's father stepped forward to recite the reflection he had written. When he had asked them if he could read the reflection they had both been taken aback. After all, he wasn't known for taking part in any ceremony outside the set royal protocols. But they had immediately agreed, touched by the gesture, if not a little apprehensive as to what he might say.

Lifting his gaze from where he stood at the lectern, he studied each of his sons in turn before saying, 'I have written a reflection on love that I would like to share with you all. "Love is found in the quiet moments. In the touch of a hand. A soothing whisper. In the acceptance of who you are. Love is holding tight in the storms of life, the willingness to change. Love is being able to say goodbye and honouring what you had. Love is generosity and forgiveness, the embracing of life. Love well, my sons and daughters. Love with joy and open hearts.'"

* * * * *